BLACk STAR

Book 4: Gods & Assassins

Frank Kennedy

Dedicated to everyone who plays second to no one.

A note from the author:

Please read the first three books of *Gods & Assassins* before you begin this tale. These books are set in the universe of the Collectorate, which includes at least two other series. Reading those series is not a prerequisite.

1

Collectorate Standard Year (SY) 5390

What's a god without many eyes? Answer: Not much of one. The merger with Ixoca brought us a step closer. In fact, I'd recommend body-sharing with a Jewel of Eternity to anyone sporting messianic ambition.

After four months of fits and starts, Moon and I saw the galaxy through hundreds of eyes, from Azteca to Amity Station to Earth. The essence of Ixoca, which he'd broken off for generations into his generals, observers, and guardians, also fell under our jurisdiction.

To be clear, this gorgeous arrangement lacked perfection. Imagine continuously watching hundreds of security monitors. At any given time, nine out of ten were filled with the mundane customs of life, while only a few tickled the ears and titillated the eyeballs. I had to learn who, when, and where to follow, all while carrying myself like a proper (and undistracted) god around my devotees.

Today, I watched from my internal control room as three lieutenants – all recipients of a piece of Ixoca – led our most important assault yet against the enemy. I despised not being at the slaughter's front line, but Ixoca reminded me of what I sometimes forgot: A god's role was to see the faithful do his bidding. Then he'd make a dramatic entrance at the perfect moment.

Ixoca proved his worth as a teacher and collaborator. So far.

I watched events unfold from an overland chaser inside the south gate of Conquillos Base, once hub of United Naval Forces operations on Azteca. The base closed fifteen years ago when the UNF downsized, but its infrastructure remained. Conquillos was an abandoned city awaiting new owners.

That temptation lured everyone here.

Commander Bett "Stopper" Ortiz spearheaded the strike against the enemy, who huddled inside the old Aztecan Central Command. Our targets were negotiating a future we intended to pause.

"Tracer," she said from her perch fifty meters from the ACC. "How's the picnic?"

Gerald "Tracer" Tolan, her second, led a team of snipers from the northwest. They entered the base overnight after we received confirmation of the meeting's locale, and hunkered down behind a cloak I devised with Ixoca's help. The same tech hid his three thousand ancient terraform shafts from surface detection. We also installed quite a beauty over Desperido.

"In position, Stopper. We have a bead on both Mary *and* Sue."

I chuckled at the coded UNF language which meant Tracer's unit could wipe out the hired help on her order.

"Standby, Tracer."

I watched Bett study her pom, which scanned ACC's interior for human movement. Our targets had arrived in flatcars and sedans, which they parked in an adjacent structure. We were all trespassers, but for one lonely Aztecan who remained at a safe distance.

"You good with this, Raul?" Bett said.

Her scan matched what I saw inside the building. Two of Ixoca's many eyes stood amid nine others gathered in a conference room. Their personal security hovered, most outside the room.

"They're sitting down to conduct business, my friend."

My words echoed in Bett's mind, courtesy of Ixoca's gift. She was one of seven 'generals' with whom Moon and I had two-way internal communication. Our original table of trust plus our top professionals – Stopper, Tracer, and Iago "Inky" Sisal – owned a piece of Ixoca.

Most of our lieutenants at first resisted the idea of gods popping into their minds on a whim (a perfectly logical response). Nor did they care for the inevitable invasion of privacy at intimate moments.

Moon and I barred ourselves from entering their minds except during military operations or when they initiated a link. In the early weeks, I fought the urge to become a voyeur. When I made a couple of 'mistakes,' they sensed my presence and called me on it.

In some ways, we became their *D'ru-shayas*. Theo had watched everything I did for centuries. Though he intervened with nasty little remarks on occasion, he kept his distance far more often than not. I exercised the same discipline.

Bett gave Tracer the order to initiate the assault.

"Say goodnight to Mary and Sue."

As soon as Tracer's team unloaded on outside security, Bett ordered her team to move in. They needed to secure the building before our targets scattered. I wanted all actors in position for the floorshow.

"Stopper, take out bit players only. Leave the masters alone to piss their pants until I arrive. Per Ixoca, no harm comes to our inside man."

"You know the drill, Raul. I run a guarantee-free zone. Those fucks don't fall to their knees, we drop them."

Damned if I didn't love this coit. Ever since the mission to Todos Santos, Bett reverted to full-on UNF killing machine. She didn't realize how much she missed it until the first engagement.

"They don't require knees to talk," I said. "If you have to, aim low. I'll be there in a jiff."

"On it, Raul."

I popped inside the youngest member of the assault team.

"Make some corpses, my friend."

Ship stood at Bett's side, loaded for hard-core business.

"I'm on it, boss."

The kid – damn, I really needed to stop calling him that – was no longer the well-meaning stumbler and bumbler under my tutelage. After I tossed him into the care of our war veterans, the kid developed an iron stomach for what had to be done. He absorbed a black eye, broken nose, and multiple kicks in the gut during the first week under Bett's regimen.

Turned out, Ship needed someone to literally beat the fear out of him. I spent too much time encouraging the little bastard.

Eh. Live and learn.

Bett's team approached the building unopposed. Tracer's quick efficiency meant the folks inside did not yet know they were in danger. Our advantage wouldn't last long.

I jumped from the chaser and straightened my apparel. Ixoca, pixelated red today, stood at my side, a projection of my mind's eye.

"What do you think, my friend? Stylish but not overstated?"

A pixelated Ixoca revealed no facial reaction to my fashionable attire, but I heard a certain relish in his voice.

"You'll haunt the prisoners," the Jewel said. "They'll know you're not to be taken lightly."

I chose a black motif. My leather vest was as dark as midnight. It disappeared inside a black triple-breasted jacket, matching pants, and a wide-brimmed hat which shaded my gorgeous mane and seductive golden eyes. The continuity broke with tinges of silver on the cuffs, polished shoes, belt buckle, and pistols.

"You know what I've missed most about godhood, Ixoca?"

"Besides the omnipotence?"

That line was always good for a stilted laugh.

"The grand entrances and the pop-ins. I couldn't get enough of those piss-your-pants moments. Humans don't know how to conduct themselves in front of a higher life form."

"They never have, Royal. Never will."

I wouldn't have expected an artificial intelligence three million years old to be such a delightful conversationalist.

"And yet we continue to give them breaks. Go figure."

"Oh, we must keep faith, Raul. A few may yet rise to the occasion. At the very least, Aztecans. That's my dream."

4

Ixoca obsessed with the Aztecan people's fate. He still sought to redeem himself for killing roundabout sixty thousand colonists ... eleven hundred years ago. Move on, already.

He knew my opinion, even if I never said the words.

"I hope these people don't disappoint you, my friend. We'll be walking a fine line in there. I'd rather not kill your favorites, but if they choose poorly, I can't allow them to walk away."

Ixoca stared at the tallest building on the base. He saw the same thing my eyes followed as Bett's team engaged our targets' security officers. It appeared the rich and underwhelming – including at least two valued members of the Children of Orpheus – took cover while their paid sacrificial lambs faced long odds.

"Understood, Raul. Assassination is a messy business. Preserve Senor Jimenez, and the rest I'll leave to your expert judgment."

On that point, we agreed. Martin Jimenez was more than mere Governor of Monteria Province and direct descendant of an original colonist. This man had his fingers in lucrative pies of all flavors, from real estate to drugs to silver mines. He stuffed the pockets of at least three cartel heads, the admin of Unified Global Shipping, and two of the planet's four reps to the Interstellar Congress.

More important, he was Ixoca's chosen to organize and unite rebel forces against the Collectorate-aligned planetary government at an appointed time. Moon and I agreed to help Ixoca set the right conditions for an insurrection; in return, he aided our goal to build a private army we'd carry far beyond this planet.

Killing Jimenez would set back both our goals.

Honestly, I was surprised President Aleksanyan hadn't targeted that malgado for assassination. Her agents pinpointed several likely Aztecan suspects in the growing "Q6 insurgency" (which was an enormous feint, courtesy of Q6 himself).

On the positive, two of his associates attending this clandestine affair *were* on the President's hit list. Moon and I acquired their names from the drop at 40-Cignus. They were cagey assholes, hard to pin down. Then Ixoca's many eyes learned of this serendipitous meeting.

We had one day to prepare and difficult decisions to make. Moon, Elian, and Genoa were already leading a team to Bolivar to set up our second off-world Motif production facility. We had promised to eliminate a crime lord and his animals in exchange for loyalty from local tribes plus guaranteed employment in our service.

After much debate, Moon and I led separate missions for the first time in our long and glorious history. If all went well (and why in ten hells wouldn't it?), we'd rendezvous in Desperido for a late dinner, followed by drinks and cigars.

With our assault at Conquillos nearly done, I told Ixoca:

"Time to run, my friend."

I removed my hat, tucked it against my side, kicked up my heels, and morphed into a blur. When I arrived at the ACC building seconds later, the final laser blast signaled an end to the fighting.

At the entrance, I patted down my slightly wind-blown hair and nestled my hat until the brim ran parallel to my eyes. Ixoca gave me the thumbs-up. He also loved the theatrics.

I sauntered through the building, filtering my perspective to two locations. Outside, Tracer's team descended from the snipers' perch. Their next task: Disposal. Upstairs, Bett's team herded survivors into a conference room with big windows.

Naturally, our captives – especially Martin Jimenez – asked the predictable questions. Who are you? What's the meaning of this? Someone with legitimate fashion sense might have also asked: Where you did buy that desert camouflage? Was it on sale?

Terrified folks never asked fun questions. Very sad.

The building ran on low-tier power, so the lifts were down. No bother. I simply followed the bodies up a stalled escalator. Three hung over the side, one with half his head blown off. They mustered a short-lived fight against highly motivated professionals.

So motivated that I spoke often with Bett about not allowing personal feelings to interfere with tactical judgment. Our targets represented the entities who shunted aside Swarm war veterans. Today's outcome demonstrated on a small scale why the powers at large wanted to marginalize these warriors.

Moon and I employed three hundred disaffected vets. Not a bad showing for four months of steady recruiting.

The corridor outside the conference room showed ample scarring from laser blasts. Other than a few blood splatters and a pair of contorted corpses, the situation appeared settled.

Two of Bett's team greeted me, including Ship. He stowed his rifle and saluted. I offered a reciprocal salute.

Bett's idea. She wanted a clear hierarchy. Salutes, chest-pounding, and secret handshakes seemed petty to me and much too human.

"Well done, my friend."

"Nothing but glitter," Ship said, emulating Elian's favorite phrase. "We cut through them like they were standup toys, boss."

"I see. And now's time for cleanup."

I reached into my jacket and found a pair of our special cigars. These were Moon's creation, but we modified them to smaller, sleeker form. Their recipe remained as potent.

Ship's eyes lit up when I handed out the cigars.

"Why don't you and Viera take care of the bodies?"

"On it, boss."

I produced a light with my index finger. The two soldiers — Viera was twenty-five years older than Ship but fit as anyone his age — puffed on the sweet leaf and proceeded to their new task.

I shouldn't have been surprised when my soldiers took a fancy to our method of quick battlefield cremation. From the first time Moon showed the little trick to Elian and Ship, they were hooked. Fire was clean, efficient, and powerful. And our humans loved the power to make a body disappear on contact.

They loved working for gods and exulted at using our tools.

As Ship set the nearest corpse ablaze, I entered the conference room. Bett and five of her team parted so I might pass.

I approached our hostages with a slow, methodical gait, all the while shifting my gaze so the seven survivors felt me in their bones. I sensed Ixoca's jealousy; he wanted to command the stage, too.

Eh. He'd have his day on a global scale. Until then, I was the star.

If these wannabe titans didn't know they were in a shitload of trouble before now, my dramatic entrance surely clarified their tenuous state of affairs. Five of the seven sat at the far end of the table. Two stood, flanking Martin Jimenez.

I greeted them a smile any mother would love.

"We're reshaping the world, are we not, senors and senora?"

I grabbed another cigar — not one of our special tools - and lit it. This was a fat bastard with a gold band, definitely Moon's favorite. He'd be honored I opened the festivities this way.

"I'll introduce myself soon enough, but I do want to allay your fear before we enter negotiations. Some of you *will live* to see the next sunrise. You have my word."

Judging by the tight jaws and nervous twitching, they didn't believe me. Frankly, two of them shouldn't have.

"Five of you matter." I shifted my gaze to the tall men in suits flanking Jimenez. "The others are mere tools on a pay stamp."

I glanced at Ixoca, and she (having turned blue and developed a feminine curvature) responded with a sharp nod. She agreed with my choice. Time for a proper display.

My mind's eye tapped into Ixoca's molecular restructuring matrix and then inside Jimenez's personal guards.

Their hearts imploded.

One collapsed onto Jimenez, who fell off his chair. The other tipped unceremoniously onto his back like an old stone sculpture.

I waited for the cries to die down and said:

"This would be a wonderful time for introductions."

2

A TRUE SHOWMAN KNEW HOW to command a stage. I practiced the art as a teen, refined it through war, and mastered the nuances after ascending. Common rabble took the bait quite easily and fell for the wow factor. Case in point: My six hundred contractors in Desperido. However, I preferred to entertain rich, self-satisfied malgados who built fortunes by sucking at the tits of the common folk.

These assholes had the furthest to fall. I afforded them the rare chance to examine just how sizeable the drop between their current lordly status and the gutter.

In my experience, few things were more emotionally satisfying than to humble privileged humans.

These five needed an extra stir before we began. I pulled on my cigar while they trembled.

"I don't like this arrangement, my friends. You're all clustered at the end. Perhaps ... yes. Let's create a more intimate setting to have a convivial conversation. Yes?"

The wide-bodied fella who should've been most terrified, given that I'd just killed his security, pushed out his chair and stood tall. He straightened his tie and glared at me with an earned indignation.

Gov. Martin Jimenez wore a silver mustache so thick it smothered his upper lip. A sprawling birthmark covered most of his left ear.

"We'll do nothing until you explain who you are and what you want."

The other four displayed none of the Governor's courage.

"Projecting strength comes naturally to you, Senor Jimenez. You built your fortune turning nasty enemies into allies. The resume is impressive. Might I point out the six rifles aimed at you, the fact that your entire security contingent is dead, and that your personal guns fell like stones. Bet you'd love to know how we did it."

He didn't miss a beat.

"Name. Now."

Jimenez made a valiant go of it.

"Commander," I told Bett. "Take Judge Barron to the back wall and shoot him in the head."

"On it."

Reynaldo Barron was a fiftysomething High Court Justice with a pin-shaped nose, wire-frame glasses, and resounding gut. He was on the President's hit list, so he'd be gone soon enough. However, he served a purpose in the upcoming negotiations. The terrified, corrupt sack of shit grabbed hold of the table, as if that would make a difference.

"No. Please. Martin, *sit down*. Now!"

Gov. Jimenez relented.

"Stop. No one else need die. What do you want of us?"

I shrugged. "You'll find I respond well to submissive behavior. Governor, why don't you take the seat directly across from me? Judge Barron, next to the Governor."

Sixty-year-old Anton Cherry, one of the five wealthiest Aztecans and a man with a decades-long chip on his shoulder, joined Barron on the President's terminal list. I asked him to flank Gov. Jimenez. He was a well-manicured gentleman who no doubt paid a personal valet to dress him in the morning. Yet his eyes failed to hide the seething rage that pursued him for the past thirty years.

When the three took their seats, I sighed.

"Quite the triumvirate." I pointed to Jimenez. "The middle-man." I doubted he appreciated my snark. To Senor Cherry, I said, "The man who would be king." Nodding to Judge Barron: "And the man who would make it all legal. What a trio."

I turned to the remaining assholes.

"Senora Sylva, sit to my left. Senor Limon to my right."

Maris Sylva, the CEO of UniShip Global (the Montez Group's chief rival), largely disappeared behind a layer cake of makeup, cherry red lipstick better suited to Desperido's care workers, and wore an orange lily over her suit jacket's lapel. No one played the commercial real estate game like Senora Sylva.

Except perhaps for a certain pair of gods who vaporized whole planets in their heyday.

Jesus Limon was chief solicitor for Esteban Poros, head of the Poros Cartel, which had been squeezed heavily of late. Poros dug into this deal as a last-ditch chance to rejuvenate his imploding empire. I empathized.

"There now," I said. "Much better. We can have a free and frank conversation as equals. People who sit at the head of a table are often drunk with power. With the exception of Senor Limon, all of us understand the allure of power. We're never satisfied. We can't rest on our laurels. Our paranoia is off the charts, as they say."

To the Governor specifically: "In response to one of your questions. What we want, like you, is to secure the future. We are here to negotiate a deal that will serve our interests and yours."

"At the end of a gun?" Jimenez sneered. "We do not negotiate with terrorists, and you are most certainly not our equal."

Time for a witty retort.

"Correct, Governor. You five come up short. As for this notion of terrorists? Yeah, no. These outstanding Aztecans joining me today protected this planet from the Swarm menace. They sacrificed so you could live free. And now, as compensation, people like you are

11

setting aside guarantees made to these heroes."

He retracted his chin with mock indignation.

"I have no idea what you mean."

"But *you* do, Senor Cherry. Records show your businesses haven't hired a veteran in fifteen years, and the last in your employ was pushed out not long after. You have a strange aversion to these warriors."

Cherry got his dander up, to no surprise.

"That's what this is about? Angry vets out for revenge?" He glared at my soldiers. "And you call us paranoid."

I chuckled. "Commander, are you here for revenge?"

"The fuck we are," Bett said in her most lilting tone. "We don't do revenge. We do justice."

"There, Senor Cherry. You see? Justice. Equal treatment under the law – both Aztecan and Collectorate. Those pro-Collectorate voices are a threat to your goals."

He started to speak, but I cut off his inevitable rant.

"Now, now. You're hardly the only violator present. Senora Sylva, what a lovely game you've played. Not only downsizing the vets at UniShip, but many who have a history of voicing their support of the young empire." She licked her cherry lips but held her tongue.

"And there's you, Judge Barron. You've worked so hard behind the scenes to toss out laws that strengthen the Collectorate's role on Azteca. Tariffs, shipping regs, environmental mandates, minimum pay stamps, vaccinations, SI investigations. And on and on."

I pointed to my proud soldiers.

"They're what you fear. When you make the big move to distance Azteca from the Collectorate, a whole army will spring up in opposition. Fighters with experience and a track record of honor. They'll remind Aztecans that without the UNF, this world was defenseless against the invaders. Once word spreads about your plot, you'll have to act fast. You'll need to overthrow the continental governments and establish a foothold before the opposition organizes. And that's where men like you, Senor Limon, come into play."

The solicitor froze. Did he expect me to overlook him? To emphasize my point, I blew a thin stream of smoke in his face.

"Men like you front the cartels. They want a piece of the action. Your employer, Esteban Poros, has promised to use his street soldiers to quell local uprisings in exchange for greater territory and a cut of the profits when Azteca goes independent. I'd reckon half the cartels made similar pledges. Yes?"

He stammered – understandable, given the jury.

"I ... I know n-nothing about such madness."

"Not to worry, Senor Limon. Everyone's in denial today. But not for long. I intend to lay out terms that will clarify our positions and, as I noted earlier, secure the future for all our interests."

Blue Ixoca crossed her so-called arms and laughed. These people were doing exactly what she wanted, setting the stage for outright rebellion. Yet she also knew they were arrogant bastards. They belonged to an oligarchy fighting a wave sure to smack them in the face. These self-indulgent cowards would hide at the first sign of trouble, demand their underlings see the work done, and take credit if the tide turned in their favor. In defeat, they'd make fast alliances with the victors to save themselves from the wall.

Ixoca knew they weren't the best bets for elevating the Aztecan people. It's why she didn't object to us killing some of them today. As long as we left Conquillos Base with certain transactions finalized, Ixoca considered a few losses to be acceptable collateral.

Oh, that Jewel of Eternity loved to play games.

I resumed. "I am going to spell out what's been happening here, my friends. You will not refute a single word because you can't. We know your plan to the nth degree. And because we're privy to the intimate details, you will wisely negotiate. Am I understood?"

I blew smoke rings while waiting for each to verbally confirm.

Huh. Hadn't done that in centuries. Interesting!

"Your plan is clever but fragile," I began. "You, Senor Cherry, want to purchase this base to use as a staging ground for your Aztecan army of independence."

I wagged a finger when he tried to object.

"You purchased many light transports and sedans with weapon mounts as well as heavy arms though your private holdings but leased them to outside operations in order to evade Collectorate law. Most leases were sold to UniShip under Senora Sylva's careful eye. The armaments were smuggled into safekeeping through the cartels, who control the night market for weapons. The Poros Cartel offered the best price – a loss leader in exchange for future benefits.

"Now, in order to acquire this base, you needed Senora Sylva's contacts in UNF Ground Operations to break down the bureaucracy. You asked Gov. Jimenez to push through a law revoking the UNF's fifty-year charter on this land. And you required Judge Barron to uphold that law by saying the charter violated the Aztecan Constitution.

"Four days ago, Senora Sylva made a deal with her UNF contact. In exchange for a considerable payment, Ground Operations will agree not to fight any effort to revoke the charter. You, Governor, plan to propose the change this week. Senor Cherry called you here to discuss not only the price he and his silent investors will pay, but their timetable to take possession of Conquillos, recruit like-minded zealots, and free this planet of the Collectorate's yoke.

"Details aside, I'd say that's a fair summation. Yes?"

Cherry would've leaped across the table to destroy me but for the rifles aimed at his head.

"How?" He seethed.

"How what?"

"How in ten hells did you ...?"

"Nope. Not today, my friend. But don't worry, Senor Cherry. No one in this room betrayed you, so far as they know."

Senora Sylva jumped into the fray with her first words.

14

"Who do you work for? We demand an answer."

"Why, I take offense. Do I look like someone who reports to a higher authority? A mere hired gun?"

Which I was, depending upon one's perspective.

"You're a murdering malgado and ..."

"Much more. None of which you'd be happy to learn. Now, let's backtrack for a moment before this show goes off the rails. Your actions would be considered treason. According to the Aztecan Constitution, treason usually means a quick death.

"My good friends with the rifles were trained to kill enemies of the Aztecan people. Commander, does anyone in your ranks have hesitation about executing these five for their crimes?"

Bett glanced to her left and right. No one on her team nodded.

"We'd prefer a jury find them guilty, but we won't lose sleep."

Ah, humans. Very easy to radicalize.

"To recap, my friends: Treason. A firing squad. No leverage. It's time for you to hear my terms and comply."

"*Your terms*?" Jimenez said. "What did you say about equals? About a convivial dialogue?"

"Oh, that? Ages ago. Now that we've established your treasonous behavior, we move into the penalty phase. Nothing congenial, convivial, or cordial about it. No, I'm going to lay out terms that might – and I emphasize *might* – allow you to leave here alive. Each of you will accept these terms and complete necessary transactions. Reach carefully into your pockets and retrieve your poms. Slowly, please. Do not open them until told."

They held their golden devices close; they must've suspected I was about to rob them blind. They were not wrong.

"Senor Cherry, you were prepared to pay fifty million UCVs for this land, while your silent investors added another thirty. Yes?"

Even staring into the face of Death, he couldn't help himself.

"Oh, I see. You intend to redirect that payment." He oozed with condescension. "You talk of these noble protectors of Azteca seeking

15

justice, but you're no more than a gang of thieves."

That brought ironic smiles to my fighters.

"Justice, my friend, is also found in monetary compensation. But yes, to the point. Of course, we're thieves. As is everyone in this room. Some thieves are more clever. Are they not?"

"You will not see one credit."

I loved how the most entitled humans carried a smugness that said, "I will always squeeze out of the tightest corner." None more so than Anton Cherry.

"You're a fascinating specimen, Senor Cherry. At an early age, you fought the Chancellors while they controlled the skies. You were coming into your own as an insurgent the same year the Chancellory fell. You and a band of enthusiasts attacked Chancellor loyalists.

"Within a year, you joined the interim government. You had a fast track toward prime minister. And then … overnight …" I fluttered my fingers like a conjurer casting a spell. "You fell. Your family's hidden connections to the Chancellors destroyed your career. Very sad."

What could he do but sneer?

"My past is not your …"

"Business? No. But I set up the past as a way to demonstrate how far you've come. You rebuilt your image by laying low, starting innovative businesses, and establishing contacts with everyone who pulled the levers of power. You followed few if any rules, and you did it in pursuit of a singular goal: A new Azteca with you on the throne. Conquillos would be your most important purchase. You wanted this for thirty years and cleared every obstacle – except my group.

"If you intend to claim this land, pay us to step aside. You are bringing eighty million to the table; that means you can afford much more. Our price is thirty million UCVs, payable immediately."

He stared at me, his conspirators, my fighters, and did the only thing any rational creature might.

Senor Cherry broke into a fit of laughter.

"Oh, of course! I'll contact my broker and have him transfer the funds. Thirty million? He'll think nothing of it."

I smiled for good measure.

"We both know you don't need a middle man. The UCVs reside in a sequestered personal account accessible through your pom. I'll provide you with my transfer point, and our business will be quick."

He rapped the table. "I assume your account is off-world and dark, so no one will be able to track the funds."

"Please open your pom and access your SPA."

"You'll have to kill me. But that will cost you dearly."

Ixoca shook her pixelated head. False bravado was a quality we both hated in humans.

Oh, well. On to the backup.

I opened my pom and searched my holos to find … ah, there it was. A live feed from a home in the city of Mantuega. A woman sat on her couch, huddled with two daughters, both less than ten.

Our third team, led by "Inky" Sisal, did well. They secured the house ten minutes before we assaulted Conquillos.

The dam collapsed around Senor Cherry when I showed him the image of his daughter and beloved granddaughters. The future king of Azteca became a blubbering heap.

"You have three minutes to transfer the funds, Senor."

As Cherry wiped his tears and fumbled to open his pom, the others laid into me.

"You filth," Jimenez said. "You would kill an innocent family for money?" The most corrupt judge on the planet said, "When you're caught, the torture will not be gruesome enough." The shipping magnate offered a feeble, "Oh, those poor little girls. Monster."

The lawyer played it cool and said nothing.

"Never make the mistake of thinking you're any better than me," I responded. "The roster of lives you people and your associates have destroyed is long and diverse. The only difference? You fill your egos with justification. I don't waste the effort."

It might have been a good time to wax philosophical about the degrees of difference between monsters. However, humans under great stress never find revelation in such moments.

I waited for Cherry to access the funds, grabbed the transfer point from my account where the President's payments also landed, and waited for confirmation. Cherry stammered.

"My ... my family ..."

When I received notice of transfer, I closed my account holo and popped inside Inky's mind, where I spoke to him.

"No more glass to break, my friend. Tell your team."

"On it, boss."

The hard part was finished. Surely, the others would fall in line.

"On behalf of Black Star," I said, "thank you for the contribution. We'll put it to good use. Now, who's next?"

3

EIGHTY DAYS EARLIER, we solved a problem while visiting the drop in 40-Cignus. I jumped out onto the asteroid after Bart detected no other ships in the star system. Only my sedan's floodlight illuminated the surface.

Ixoca emerged alongside in full human form, exemplified by the best of both genders.

"I haven't visited a dead system in three-quarters of a million years," the Jewel told me in a wistful tone. "We were searching for the final planets, my brethren and I."

We strolled apace to the fissure where a titanium casement stored the memglass detailing the President's next assignment.

"That's a long gap, my friend. How far were you from Azteca?"

"In Collectorate time? Four thousand standard years. The journeys were slow, but our patience was infinite and our goals concrete." The Jewel turned into the floodlight. "Might we have a moment of natural light only?"

"Sure. How about it, Moon?"

My optical sensors adjusted to find the tiniest ambient light amid a sea of darkness. What emerged beyond was truly spectacular; a view I took for granted all those centuries.

"Stunning, isn't it?" Ixoca said. "The stars. The nebulas. The gases. Layers of black matter, raw and naked. A portrait without an artist. Gods, Jewels, and humans think of ourselves as conquerors, explorers, and inventors."

"Aren't we?"

"Only to the extent we manipulated the tiniest nanofraction of this portrait. Our impact can only be quantified on a microscopic scale."

"Huh. That's a blow to the ol' ego, my friend. What about you, partner? Was our impact microscopic?"

Moon laughed. He did that more often after Ixoca entered our lives.

"We sealed the bridges between universes and shifted reality. Sounds to me like success on a macro level."

The Jewel apologized.

"I speak of the visible universe as originally constructed. Your work with Royal was profound, but it did little to alter the architecture that emerged from the Great Fire. Perhaps the god who banished you, this *Father and Mother* you speak of, may offer a different perspective."

Moon and I had a good chuckle.

"Doubtful we'll ever hear from *Father and Mother,*" I said. "It paid attention to us when It had no choice and left a parting gift. If I had to speculate, I'd say It no longer gives ten hells about any of us."

I didn't believe that anymore, but I wanted Ixoca to believe.

"Consider that a bonus, Royal. The artist is not as important as the art. This is perfection. A canvas of forever."

Subjective interpretation, of course, but I saw his point.

"Everything begins and ends in the black, my friend?"

"Indeed. The molecular heartbeat dances and sings uninhibited inside this ocean. Light is a distraction. Organic and artificial life are ephemeral, bound by laws both natural and manufactured. But the ocean goes on. It will exist after the Dying Light. It has no name, nor does it crave one. It always was, always will be. Perfection."

Now that's what I called one chatty Jewel.

20

"Moon, lights please."

We proceeded to the casement, which I opened to discover the memglass. Inside, names of the fools we'd assassinate next.

"So," I told Ixoca, reflecting on his poetic stroll, "if the universe is a single organism, as you suggest, then everything in the visible spectrum is mere decoration."

The gender-neutral Jewel forced a sly grin.

"We serve at its pleasure."

"Toying with us, you believe?"

It nodded. "Forever cloaked."

"More powerful than *Father and Mother?*"

"Unsurpassed."

Felt like a stretch. We didn't continue the conversation inside Bart. Rather, we examined the memglass and its reports on our multiple Aztecan targets.

Thanks to the trip, I solved a problem. Our group needed a proper name; Ixoca provided the spark.

I announced it to the table of trust.

"Black Star. We will be everywhere but hide in plain view. Anyone who shines their light upon us will be absorbed into the endless ocean." I carried my message to our growing army. "Not bound to the laws and limitations which make a mockery of short life. Our name will be celebrated and feared. Like the universe itself."

Who wouldn't applaud and cheer such a provocative declaration? Our fighters let rip. They embraced the name but treated it with the same care as the Children of Orpheus among their own kind.

Except we weren't a cult. We wore no tattoos, said no pledges, but understood what lay ahead: The freedom of utter chaos. What better place to gather all those in search of a thing than Desperido?

So, when I thanked Senor Cherry for the last great deed of his life, I spoke our group's name because he deserved to know who brought him to his end.

Did the wannabe king suspect he had signed his death warrant at the same moment he freed his daughter and grandchildren? Hard to tell. He was funeral gray and showed none of the false bravado.

"To you, Gov. Jimenez. We're not interested in your money. We could drain you for thirty million, and you'd follow Senor Cherry's lead."

Was that relief I detected in his long, deep exhale?

"Then what?"

"You are going to resign your office."

Those tight jaws said he didn't see that one coming.

Moments such as this were a genuine breath of fresh air.

"Why would I ever ...?" He cut himself off with a sudden look of recognition. "What have you done to my family, you mal ...?"

"Settle, Governor. Settle. Submit your resignation to Parliament and recommend Deputy Minister Alton Braga replace you."

"Wuh ...? Braga? Why?"

"Because he's the most pro-Collectorate voice in the continental governments. My friends with the rifles will appreciate that. And because if you don't, your considerable stake in the Poros, Minghella, and Ochoa cartels' drug trade will be exposed. Tonight.

"Your fall will be slow and torturous, and your legacy annihilated. Take our deal, and you walk away as a civilian, your fortune intact."

Jimenez was nobody's fool. He smelled subterfuge.

"That's all? With everything I've seen today, you won't simply allow me to walk."

"Actually. Yes. I will. Oh, we'll keep tabs on you. The first time you speak of this gathering, try to hunt us down, or reassert your authority, we'll kill your entire extended family."

Cherry, sitting beside Jimenez, must have felt like the world's biggest chump. The inequity of the punishment no doubt clawed at him. I'd put him out of that misery soon enough.

Jimenez persisted.

"No one will believe it. Too many questions will be asked. I have no reason to leave. I have been Governor for thirteen years."

22

"That's a good reason, my friend. If not, make up an excuse. You're tired. You're sick. Time for a fresh point of view. But you will submit formal notice to Parliament within the hour."

Ixoca and I debated the Governor's fate for days. This man wore two of Ixoca's many eyes all his life. The Jewel said he was once a promising member of the cause. He would be again – but as a civilian. Jimenez would use anger and resentment to work in the shadows building stronger alliances against the pro-Collectorate governments than he ever could as a statesman.

Frankly, I didn't know Jimenez and decided to trust Ixoca's judgment. The Jewel said momentum toward the insurgency would not be lost, only set back by a few months. And the short-term solution would please the soldiers of Black Star.

Compromise. A difficult goddamn word, but not outside my working vocabulary.

"Judge Barron, you too have a document to submit, but it won't be your resignation."

The wide-bodied jurist loosened his collar.

"What document?"

I retrieved it from my pom, expanded the holo to a nice, readable screen, and hurled it at him.

"For years, you have worked with the Governor and other like-minded rapscallions to undermine Azteca's relationship to the Collectorate. You used the planet's Constitution like a bullwhip to set the stage for Aztecan independence. That ends now.

"This document, which we have crafted for you, is both a legal determination and a confession. You have seen the error of your ways. You succumbed to the influence of xenophobic hardliners in rendering your decisions. No more. You now freely admit that Collectorate laws do not impose suffering on the Aztecan economy. You call for a full review of all High Court decisions on these issues. All you need to do is sign and deliver."

He glared at the words like they were written in a foreign

23

language. His lips downturned and his nose sniffed a turd.

"No. Like Gov. Jimenez said, no one will believe it. The statement contradicts ten years of my rulings. I will be accused of corruption. And at any rate, it has no legal binding. These are recommendations."

"Which should work to new Gov. Braga's advantage. Yes?"

"No. I will never be trusted again."

"May be. That's why you're going to send a second statement to your office staff." I hurled it his way. "In light of your conversion, you have decided to take a one-month leave to refocus and reenergize. You ask all parties to respect your privacy during the absence."

Barron saw through me, as did the others.

"A month? You intend to make me disappear. You intend to kill me."

"Not at all. Two of my people will take you to a private location and watch after you. It's a lovely retreat in the Sesquina Mountains. They'll allow you to contact your family under certain conditions."

I hurled bullshit wrapped in a dulcet tone. My favorite.

The moment I saw Barron's name on the President's hit list, he was a dead man. Yet Moon, Ixoca, and I thought his departure opened some interesting doors. As such, we'd send him off with Tracer and one other fighter. They'd take him to a lovely cabin in the Sesquinas, stage a suicide but leave bread crumbs suggesting murder.

The inevitable investigation would uncover circumstantial evidence tying Special Intelligence to the killing. A scandal would erupt, calling into question the sudden change in the governor's office and foul play by the Collectorate. Oh, the conspiracy theorists would have a field day, lending a touch of fuel to the independence movement.

By then, if all went to plan, Black Star would be based off world.

Serving different interests proved a fascinating puzzle to solve.

Barron resisted for a short while. Then I showed him current images of his family.

24

Really, was there any better ploy than threatening the lives of loved ones? It was simple and somewhat cliché in the grand picture but also a classic strategy. Sometimes, men like me overthought.

Simplify. Streamline.

I sent the judge away with his escorts. He whimpered into the corridor. Oh, yes. He knew.

That left me with the least interesting of the five.

"Senora Sylva, you are the queen of commercial real estate. But I'm afraid, like with the three senors, you'll have to suffer a humbling setback. With the Governor, the King Wannabe, and the Judge out of the picture, you're in a bind.

"I'll need you to communicate that difficulty with your contacts in UNF Ground Operations. You'll have to not only back out of that rather large bribe, but you'll request the UNF establish a limited presence on Conquillos. You'll say the forces willing to purchase this land planned to overthrow the duly elected government."

Appalled didn't begin to describe her reaction. Was it possible for the cherry lipstick to suddenly turn a pale pink? Her tears validated an eternal truth: Heavy makeup and water did not blend well.

Yet I don't think she feared me as much as she did Anton Cherry, who had regained a fair bit of his composure.

Treachery in the ranks. Oh, the horror.

"Did you ...?" Sylva rubbed her hands together. Improvising, perhaps. Or just a nervous cunt with no way out. "Did you also write my message?"

"Oh, no. You'll be recording and sending the message in a few moments. We'll escort you to a separate room."

"If I do this, I'm good as dead. When the UNF lands here, my associates will know it was me." She pointed to Cherry. "He knows."

Cherry wasn't smug. He'd just been swindled out of thirty million credits, a tiny portion of his assets. I'm sure he still intended to claim this base over time.

"Do as he says, Maris. I know the truth. You'll be protected."

25

Sounded like a man who thought he'd see tomorrow.

Because she had no spine, Senora Sylva conceded. By this point, Tracer and his unit completed cleanup. He entered the room.

"Fine job, my friend." I pointed him out to the four hostages. "Another man who sacrificed for Azteca."

"We're ready to leave with the judge," Tracer said.

"Outstanding. Follow protocol. Make him comfortable. Yes?"

"On it, boss."

"You see, Senora? We're not monsters, but we are doers. And you have a task. Commander, please escort the lovely lady down the hall to construct her message for the UNF."

"On it."

No one here would ever see Senora Sylva again. Bett had orders to kill the woman after she transmitted her message. As head of UniShip, Sylva put more veterans out of work than Montez ever did.

Cold-blooded murder wasn't Bett's game. Not at first. She wanted justice, yes. She despised how the planet's major institutions slowly turned against its saviors.

Yet she also valued honor. Killing enemy combatants could be justified. An execution by a self-appointed judge and juror? No.

So, we talked at great length. Alone and over many drinks.

"Honor is not a state of being," I said. "It's bred for the moment. A product of context. Don't waste it on those who don't deserve it."

In time, she came around.

Three fighters remained with us as I finished my business.

"Senor Limon, return to your employer and deliver a message. Tell Esteban Poros to transfer all weapons being held for Senor Cherry to the Horax. His friend Mateo Cardinale will assume responsibility."

I used *friend* with considerable irony. Poros and Cardinale despised each other. As usual, it had something to do with a woman.

"You can persuade him on legal grounds. Say he will no longer have the protection of, well ..." I pointed to the men across the table. "Better the Horax assume the liability. Yes?"

Limon nodded sharply. This fella was no dummy.

"Senor Poros will want compensation."

"You can negotiate a fair price with Cardinale. He's lost considerable territory and street soldiers in the past few months."

Mostly on our account.

"Anything else?"

"Nope. I'd say you have the simplest task. Go back to soliciting for Senor Poros and say nothing of what happened here."

Limon must've thought he was getting out of Conquillos like a bandit. He was blessed not to have great power. Otherwise, I would have sliced his carotid with a thought.

Of course, he'd tell Poros what happened. Of course, Poros wouldn't sell the entire armory. Of course, Cardinale wouldn't make a fair offer. Of course, there'd be bad blood. Of course, there'd be war between the two cartels. Of course, the war would spread.

A perfect symphony of chaos.

I shouted for Ship. The kid returned in a cloud of cigar smoke.

"Please escort Senor Limon to his vehicle."

"No worries, boss."

I grabbed Limon as he rose.

"First, your pom. I'm sure Senor Poros will buy you another."

The man did not hesitate. He knew the score.

After they departed, I studied Jimenez and Cherry, the assholes who vowed to change Azteca forever. Given time, Jimenez might even succeed; but I'd be long past caring by then. I directed them to turn over their poms as well.

"I'm sure you have all manner of titillating data buried beneath your identity stamp. Isn't it fun how we store so much of ourselves in our technology?" I dropped the pocket-watch style devices in my jacket. "And yes, yes. I know. They're worthless to me. No way to penetrate the genetic signature."

That wasn't true anymore. Ixoca showed me a few tricks.

"I thank you both for your time. Humans have long aspired to

Frank Kennedy – Black Star

climb mountains for the sheer sake of saying they did. Some have fallen along the way. And some are unworthy."

Jimenez pounded the table. About time someone demonstrated a little spine.

"Enough! You won. *Today*. Tell us who you are."

Eh. He bored me.

"You're free to go, Governor. One of my men will follow you. Simply leave the building, enter your sedan, and drive away. You know what must be done. We are with you always. If word has not reached us of your resignation within the hour ..."

His gears turned. What mighty twists and turns could he employ to save himself and everyone in his orbit? He'd scheme until a few kilometers outside the base, when Ixoca would pop into his mind and set him straight. Then the last resistance would fall.

So departed the best of the worst. I ordered the last two guards to surround Cherry.

"You were always the one I wanted to meet. Few men have ever tried to change history by taking control of it. Far fewer succeeded. Come, Senor Cherry. Let's speak outside. A few parting words."

Even with rifles pressed against him, Cherry wouldn't budge.

"I demand answers."

"You'll have them. But if you don't move, these Aztecan heroes will execute you for your crimes. Do you want to live?"

Of course he did. Very sad.

4

CHERRY FOLLOWED ME down a long corridor, flanked by a continuous window. I wanted him to make a move against me. Fight for his damn life. Eh. It would've been suicide, but at least he'd have gone out on his own terms. Not enough humans appreciated the value of such an ending.

"Do you know what happens after you're gone?" I asked.

When Cherry didn't answer, I moseyed to the window and admired the scenery. Conquillos felt much more expansive.

I pulled on my cigar, now half smoked.

"Simple question, Senor Cherry. What happens after death?"

He studied me then the two fighters who lingered.

"If you plan to kill me ..."

"The question, Senor. Answer."

Typical of a lazy mind, he said:

"I don't know."

"Never thought of it?"

"Everyone does."

"It's the great question, isn't it? The answer is out of reach for the living. Or so it would seem."

He balled a pair of fists. *Come on, Cherry. Do it!*

"You claim to know the secret?"

29

"I do. See, I was born immortal. I've died so often ... oh, I lost count long ago. But I'm not an Aeternan. I'm better."

I removed a black leather glove and allowed Ixoca's blue essence to shine through my palm. He stumbled backward.

"W-what are you?"

Such a disappointing response. They always asked the same cudfrucking question. Why not something original? For once, couldn't someone say, "Nice. Where can I get some of that?"

Nope. Lazy, lazy.

"I'm two thousand years old. Although honestly? Seems like yesterday I was a kid living in the sewer. The answer to what lies beyond is terrifying, Senor Cherry. It's an abyss into which all your psychoses are poured. Life taunts you. To die is to despair.

"I never endured more than fifteen minutes of it before I regenerated. When I returned to the living, I felt as if someone had been suffocating me with a pillow. Life is the only peaceful part of our great journey, Senor."

Did he believe me? Did I care?

"Look out there, Senor. Twenty years ago, your people flooded this base with willing volunteers to fight humanity's greatest existential threat. What were you doing at the time?"

"Helping our people in any way I could."

His lips crinkled under the lie.

"You say the words with a straight face. The only one you helped was yourself. You formed a group that insisted the Swarm were an imaginary enemy, a mere pretext for the UNF to establish a permanent foothold, like the Chancellors before them. You advocated for open rebellion even then. Wish I'd seen the look on your face when the Swarm fleet crossed the divide from Beta Universe."

At that moment, Anton Cherry studied me in a different light. Something I said clicked. A truth buried behind rumor and legend. His cheeks fell with the sudden recognition.

He knew.

Finally, somedamnbody made the connection.

"You're one of *them*."

I snickered. "One of what?"

"The stories about the Swarm ... The Wave. How it all ended."

"Only now do you put it together. You must feel silly. Thirty years of maneuvering to claim something that never belonged to you in the first place. Senor, no human is meant to stand above all others. That honor, my friend, is reserved for gods."

"No. You're ..."

He didn't need to speculate any further. Even my trusted table hadn't been told the whole truth. If anyone knew precisely who Moon and I were, they had yet to step forward. We often debated whether to admit we were their saviors.

"Speaking of people who are too big for their pants, I have a message from the President. Time for you to suffocate."

I went old school.

Yes, it was quicker and quieter to use Ixoca's gift to destroy a man from within, but it lacked special effects.

I threw Cherry against the outer window, whipped out both my pistols, and shot six times.

Each laser bolt hit its target (I never missed). The glass shattered in six places around Cherry, who stared at me in disbelief. He wasn't dead. Maybe there was still a chance. Maybe ...

"No worries, my friend. I'll always be with you. The abyss will see to it."

Seconds before I shot six laser bolts into his chest, I shapeshifted through all the assassins who had done the President's bidding. Unlike the past, when a shift was painful and tiring, Ixoca gave me the strength to move between forms in the blink of an eye.

I reshifted into Raul while the wannabe King of Azteca fell through the shattered glass.

Ixoca and I looked over the edge and studied the twisted corpse. The Jewel pixelated red.

"Do you behave this way with everyone you assassinate?"

"There's usually not time for theatrics, my friend. Quick in, quick out." I flicked my cigar through the opening. "But I do enjoy seeing the last light in their eyes. I love when they deny it to the final nanosecond. Yep. Discovered that joy when I was still a kid."

"I'd love to hear more about your early days."

"No, you wouldn't. I'm sure you witnessed more than a few garden-variety serial killers over the past thousand years."

"Yes, but I never had the pleasure to merge with one."

The fighters approached, asking for instructions.

"Rendezvous with Commander Ortiz. She should be finished by now. Make sure we've taken care of all cleanup. The remaining personal vehicles will have to be removed and destroyed."

"On it, boss."

They turned on a dime. We watched them disappear around the corner toward the room where Bett had taken the late Senora Sylva. Ixoca crossed his apparent arms and sighed.

"I find it comforting how nonchalant these soldiers behave in your presence, Royal. They accept you without reservation."

"You expected different?"

"Yes. I long feared Aztecans would not embrace me after my truth became public knowledge. You've shown that the resistance will likely be minimal."

"Timing, my friend, is pivotal. You heard Cherry's last words. He mentioned The Wave. Every human knew the event changed their perspective at some level, but most couldn't articulate how."

"I was immune to its effects, Royal."

"But not your disciples. Follow me."

I jumped out the window and landed like a feather next to the pool of blood spreading from Cherry's shattered skull.

"This asshole only acknowledged the truth when he had nothing left to face. There will always be some like him. Most humans no longer wear blinders. The Wave shifted their connection to the

32

universe. At some level, they're prepared to accept a hard truth about our hierarchy."

"What truth?"

"Humans walk. Gods run. It's the natural order."

"Yet the two can exist in harmony."

"I wouldn't call it symbiotic, but it's a simple relationship."

Ixoca bent down and studied the corpse.

"Until my people know the whole truth, it will not be so simple. The things we've done today will reverberate."

"Oh, yes. One doesn't kill power players and expect everyone else to sleep on it. Of course, that's part of the fun."

Ixoca's raucous laughter filled my mind with an uneasy vibe. It echoed with the verve of a true megalomaniac. A full-on lunatic. An actor who didn't realize less was more. Either it was an affectation, or the Jewel was tone deaf.

"We've introduced many new variables, Royal. Watch carefully in the coming days. Sands will be shifting. The wrong eyes might turn to Desperido sooner than you anticipated."

"Always a risk, my friend. Calculated but necessary. We made thirty-eight million UCVs today. Eight will arrive in my account as soon as I confirm these kills to the President's people."

"You could've made much more."

Moon leveled the same point when I determined the amount to extort from Cherry.

"Preparations, patience, and poise, my friend. An empire is not built in a day or on the back of one man's bank account."

"I see. A thief must know his limitations."

"A good one always does. The others have short careers."

We returned to the overland chaser, but I monitored both teams as they completed cleanup. Tracer and the judge traveled to the Sesquina Mountains. Judge Barron whimpered like a little boy who couldn't get his way.

Poor Tracer. I almost told him to put the judge out of his misery, but a premature death complicated the suicide setup. Ixoca, Moon, and I agreed: If evidence didn't point to SI agents, murdering him in elaborate fashion held no purpose.

I switched gears.

"Stopper, everything good with Sylva?"

"Book's closed on that one, boss. She dictated a credible message. Not sure if the Admiralty will give credence to her theory about an insurrection, but it wouldn't shock the fuck out of me if they sent a few investigators. They've gotta cover their ass."

"And the execution?"

She rendezvoused with her teams.

"Did her myself, boss. Made certain that cunt damn well knew why."

"Well done. With any luck, the next chairman of UniShip will look more kindly upon Azteca's warriors. In the meantime, I'm going to meet Ixoca's contact about his ship. Try not to be too long. I'd love your input before I make a purchase."

She stifled a laugh.

"If this baby's anything like the man describes, I'm sure it's a piece of shit and exactly what we're looking for. See you there."

The man in question was Carlos Aylet, the primary caretaker of Conquillos. He was once a UNF quartermaster based there; he hung around until they turned off the lights. The UNF paid him a stipend along with his pension to provide token security, which meant monitoring drones and secure cams.

He was also, much to our lovely good fortune, a guardian for the Children of Orpheus. Ixoca encouraged him to black out the internal security all day and expect visitors in the afternoon.

Carlos greeted me outside a humble white abode that used to function as base annex, three hundred meters across the plateau. My eyes set upon the adjacent warehouse. Carlos wasn't much to look at: Sloppy, wasted, a man with no friends and family. But, from what I'd been told, skilled with phasic tools and obsessed with restoring classics.

"Raul Torreta." I offered him a cigar, which he greedily accepted after smelling the leaf. "I represent a consortium named Black Star. We're interested in your vessel."

He gave me the once-over.

"Black Star? Just so's we understand, Senor Torreta: If it's your intent to junk her for parts, we got's no sale, and you'll kindly leave my land."

Carlos wasn't rude. He sounded like a protective dad. Still, I didn't appreciate reluctant salesmen.

"Technically, I believe this is UNF property, but let's not devolve into semantics. If the vehicle is what you describe, and it's space-worthy, I'll tender an offer today."

He raised his hands.

"Now no sense jumping afore you can leap. Wanna see her?"

"I'm not here for cake and gossip."

Carlos didn't have much to his frame and a steady limp off his left foot. Outside the warehouse cargo door, he sported a grin.

"I'd reckon that was you lot down to the base."

"Could be. How close were you looking?"

"Me? Neh. I don't keep an eye on the place lessen the drone flash a breach warning. And she's been running inactive for twelve hours now. If you take my meaning."

"I take, Carlos. The ship, if you please."

He pulled back the massive door to reveal what at first resembled a discombobulated workshop rather than a warehouse. Crates stacked on top of each other, random sections of hull plating lay in piles, and an overhead light flickered to an annoying buzz. But we didn't have to walk far to see the prize.

A crab-shaped transport three times larger than Bart dominated the central workspace. Ladders scaled it like so much scaffolding, but the hull was intact. The design flooded me with memories.

"A UG Scramjet. Vintage Collectorate era."

Carlos nodded.

"Serial tracker indicates it came off the line in 5344."

"Fourteen years before the Chancellory fell. How did you acquire it?"

"I didn't, so to speak." He dropped his hands to his hips and admired the beautiful ship as he explained. "Conquillos was a staging ground for the Unification Guard long afore the UNF come along. They left in a hurry when their Carriers were undone. Best I can make out, this girl were undergoing repairs to her Carbedyne nacelles. No time to make her space-worthy. She was orphaned."

I first experienced aerial combat inside a ship of similar make.

"You're telling me she's been sitting here for thirty-two years?"

"All of it. The UNF used a few repurposed Scramjets in the early days, till their new fleet was up to par. But never her. Not my Maria."

"Maria?"

"After my mother. If you buy Maria, name her as you please."

In terms of capacity, Maria fit our needs.

"Is the ship viable for flight?"

"She'll go. All she's lacking is ninety liters of full-flush Carbedyne accelerant. Hard to find on today's market, for sure, but a man like yourself has people in the know. Yes?"

Less glorious memories returned.

"I remember those days, my friend. We struggled with supply chain issues for Carbedyne G-up. But yes, I have a network. I'll stay ahead of the need."

"I thought about removing the Carbedyne flush tunnels and shifting out for Carbedyne fins — more efficient and modern, you see. But it's hard on a pension."

"Hmm. This is what you've done with yourself all these years? Fiddle with the ship?"

He waved me forward to the port egress.

"Got no family. The world leaves me alone. UNF don't mind what I do with her."

"They don't care if you sell Maria?"

We started up the ramp.

"She ain't even in the registry. I removed the Guard transponder. Maria's a forgotten relic."

"Huh. Unregistered. Off book."

"I'd wager that's an attractive quality."

"Perfect."

The cabin stunned me. All components shined as if fresh off the assembly line. Long banks of Recon tubes on either side of the bulwark, two rows of still-seats, and a dozen swivels in the forward compartment. And that up front ... was it a ...?

"Standalone Nav circle. Haven't seen one in twenty years."

The navigator's still-seat pivoted inside a cylindrical shield, where he'd control the ship through kinetic holographs.

"The best of all designs," Carlos said. "Chancellors used them for two centuries. The newer systems are fine, but they do nothing to improve efficiency."

I crossed universes in a Scramjet all but identical to this one.

"Have you updated the programming matrix?"

"Where I can."

Ixoca interjected a thought.

"You and I have the capacity to resolve any limitations."

"Agreed."

"What's that, now?" Carlos asked.

"Ah. Nothing. When we're able, we'll take her for a spin and tweak as needed."

No point asking about a wormhole drive. These old models predated that tech by decades. They used the Fulcrum for intersystem journeys. We wouldn't need long to integrate a new, illegal drive.

"Weapons package?"

"Intact for the most part. A clever man can find what he needs on the night market."

Bett and her top lieutenants arrived soon after. They had mixed feelings. The ship brought back childhood memories, when the Chancellors ruled the forty worlds. Scramjets appeared planetside bearing invincible warriors in red body armor, the peacekeepers.

The unregistered bit changed Bett's mind in a hurry.

"You said you were looking for a flagship, boss. You found her."

Bett was right.

"A new coat of paint on the hull, a few other mods, and we'll be set, my friends. Carlos, if we provide the Carbedyne, how soon can you make her ready?"

"By myself, now?" He reference the limp. "If I had helping hands, we could clear Maria in three, four days."

Interesting.

"Price?"

"Eh, oh. If I made back what I put in her plus ten percent, you'd make me a happy man. Though I'd so hate to say goodbye to her."

A cheap bastard would wait until Maria was flight-approved then kill Carlos. We'd leave here with a ship no one knew existed.

Yeah, no.

Carlos weren't much to look at, but he'd put his goddamn heart and soul into this vessel. Here was a man with patience and persistence.

We shook on a price, but that wasn't enough.

"You've been alone too long, Senor Aylet. Might you be interested in a new career?"

5

WE LEFT THREE VOLUNTEERS behind to expedite the work on our new Scramjet. I wanted that beauty in Desperido ASAP to start worm drive modifications. Our terrestrial fleet had grown tenfold in the past four months, but Bart remained our only private link to the stars.

Before we departed the base annex, I pulled Bett aside.

"Great work today, Stopper. Both teams will receive stipends. The usual cut."

She lit a cheroot, her tradition after every mission.

"Appreciated, boss."

"Maria will be a game-changing asset. We need more like her."

Bett pushed smoke through a corner crease in her lips.

"Those old warhorses are hard to find. The UNF destroyed or repurposed practically everything the Guard flew."

"So I've heard. Without Ixoca's eyes, we wouldn't have found Maria. We need to expand our range."

Bett scratched under her good eye, a tic signaling worry.

"You want me to reach out beyond Azteca."

"Only to old friends who might have something to offer. Did you develop relationships with anyone in engineering or Nav?"

"Believe it or not, Raul, back then I was a regular people person. I was up in everydamnbody's business. Then it went to hell and ..."

We covered this ground often. Bett's memory of service blossomed after she regained the thirst for combat. How many nights inside the cantina did she share war stories while outdrinking her fighters?

"You tried to put it behind. Yes. Many of your comrades faced the same conflicts. Like some Aztecan vets, they might also have chosen unsavory career paths. Smuggling, for instance. Anyone in the night market could advance our cause."

She didn't put up a fight laced with profanities. Bett hadn't lost her foul mouth. Rather, she respected the chain of command, and Commander MaryBeth Ortiz reported to me and Moon.

"I'll get on it soon as we're home, boss. But I have to warn you: It's been over ten years for some of my old mates. For all I know, they'll be in the wind, if they ain't dead."

"No need to perform miracles."

"You're looking for unregistered, Raul, and that's best of both worlds. But it ain't practical on our timetable."

"Agreed. We have the funds to add to our fleet through legal sellers, but I don't want to overextend until our operations on Bolivar and Inuit are running at full capacity."

She finished the cheroot with one overlong puff and stamped it beneath a shoe.

"You know my concern. If we're forced into a full evac ..."

"We won't have the capacity. Well aware, Stopper. I'll pull the trigger on Bart lookalikes before our situation becomes dire."

"Speaking of, what's the latest from Bolivar?"

I shifted my many eyes across the light-years to see through Moon and Elian. My partner advanced with Genoa under cover of night, surveying the fortifications of a mountain lodge that housed a crime lord we promised to put down. Elian sat at Bart's Nav, preparing a firing solution to lay waste to the lodge's outer walls.

"They'll attack soon."

"Moon chose a good team. They'll burn those motherfuckers."

Bett's increasing relish for murder demonstrated the lack of moral ambiguity I needed from my army. As long as every enemy evoked the same focused anger as the Swarm, she'd remain an effective commander.

We left in separate vehicles. I could have loaded my chaser into the back of our troop transport, which was about half the size of a Scramjet and barebones but for the modified Carbedyne fins.

However, I preferred a quiet albeit longer journey in Red Dust. Upgrades to her fuel infusion system increased her velocity by fifty percent. I'd return to a crowded Desperido in four hours; solitude was harder to find these days.

As I hopped into the forward bucket, Ship joined me on the passenger side. *Shit.* I'd forgotten about the kid's pre-mission request to ride along. Something about an important decision he reached. Even if I had used Ixoca's many eyes to become a voyeur, I couldn't have read Ship's thoughts ahead of time.

"Still OK with this, boss? If you changed your mind, I'll ..."

"No, no, my friend. Make yourself comfortable. Be warned: I'll max out the accelerator. We'll reach two-forty kph in five seconds."

Ship whistled as he strapped in.

"Sure she can handle it, boss? That's mad flying."

"Be more concerned about yourself. We won't fly on a level plane, and there are no vomit bags."

I entered our course into the Nav, which had been upgraded to a proper AI with holo tools. The initial acceleration did not impact me, of course, but it threw most humans for a disorienting jolt. The world passed by us in a blur.

The combination of a screaming engine and steady vibration did not create the best environment for personal banter. So, I lowered my auditory sensors and popped into Ship's mind.

"The fighting on Bolivar will start soon," I said. "Don't take offense if I appear distracted."

He'd gotten used to hearing my dulcet tones inside his head. Ship learned how to respond with a calm, twelve-inch voice.

"No problem, boss. I'm just as excited. Keep me filled in."

"Will do, my friend. Now, what is this important decision you wanted to discuss?"

He hesitated. When I glanced into the passenger bucket, Ship kept his giant oval eyes focused dead ahead. Did he have second thoughts?

"I'm waiting, Ship."

"Oh. Sorry, boss. It's just … I've been thinking about it for weeks. Reckon now's the time. I proved myself to you, right?"

"As a soldier or a man?"

"Both, I hope."

One was complicated. The other, not so much.

"Stopper says you stand toe to toe with men more than twice your age. She says you don't back down anymore. And I heard a rumor: You spend many nights sharing your bed with a delicate creature."

The kid snickered.

"A rumor, boss? You mean you don't peek? I just assumed …"

"We gave our word, Ship. How could you follow me if I betrayed your trust?"

"Yeah. Good point."

"Besides, I hate to watch amateurs engage in intercourse. It's sloppy. The cadence is off, and the orgasm is never up to par."

After a moment of embarrassment, Ship saw through my snark and burst into laughter.

"You had me going, boss. I can't believe I waited so long for sex. I used to ask Lumen if I could pay a care worker, but she always said no. Some shit about customer relations."

"She did have the anti-Carib bias to consider. Lumen was looking out for you."

"I know. Sometimes … I can't believe I'm saying it, but some days I actually miss her."

"Not surprising. You shared that cantina with her for five years.

And, as it turns out, she did save your life."

Lumen told Moon and me the story of precisely how she did it right before the old cunt left Desperido for good. She asked me to pass along the truth of how Ship ended up in the anus of Azteca. How the boy was thrust upon her in a night-market deal gone wrong, and how the smugglers would have spaced him had she refused to purchase the kid.

"That's more or less what I need to talk about, boss. Not Lumen, but how I wound up in the night market."

I kept my promise to Lumen and passed along her story a day after she departed. At the time, Ship handled the truth with a quiet dignity but spoke little of it afterward.

"I hope you don't wish to find Lumen and thank her. She's not interested in Desperido or you. Not anymore."

"No, boss. I'm ready to make things right with my family."

Huh. Didn't expect that.

"A reunion on Everdeen?"

"Not as such. All those years, I thought my family tossed me out, but it wasn't their fault. I want the assholes responsible to pay."

"How?"

"I aim to kill them."

"Ah. Do you know their identities?"

"No, but my parents do."

"So, you'll return to Everdeen, take down names, and stalk the perpetrators until you slaughter them one by one. Yes?"

"Will you help me?"

"That's a big ask, my friend."

"You're an assassin, Raul. You've been doing this sort of thing for years."

"Longer than you realize."

"You told me what happened when you were a teen on Hokkaido. How your lover was murdered in an ambush, and you stalked the killers one at a time. You can give me pointers."

43

That remark elicited a faint chuckle.

"Pointers, my friend? One does not train for serial slaughter. Now, I must admit: You have become a fine, efficient killer under Bett's tutelage. You're steady with a rifle, and you step outside your fear. But there is a notable difference between the business of murder and a quest for revenge."

"Which is?"

"The latter produces no satisfaction. It's a trap, my friend. It becomes an obsession. You lose sight of pragmatic concerns and carry a false notion that when you finish, you will find fulfillment. Revenge teaches you only how to become a monster. How all your problems can be solved with murder. I learned this lesson once."

"Did it stop you from killing people?"

"No, but now I do it for a combination of profit and pleasure. I have no compelling need to scratch an unsatisfying itch."

He didn't know the tenth of it. If Moon and I wanted revenge for how the Collectorate treated us after our heroic deeds, we would've lost our minds in the first years of exile, left the Fort of Inarra, and killed everyone in our path. Regardless of culpability.

"So, you're saying you won't help me?"

"Ship, you're asking me to divert time and resources to a planet where we have no vested interest to help you fulfill a revenge fantasy. It's not efficient or cost-effective, and there's no guarantee you walk out of there alive. Why do you care what happens to those people? I'm quite sure they've long since forgotten you."

"I hope so. Their guard will be down. They won't expect me."

"Assuming they still walk free. Ship, these people were engaged in The Trade. Again, I ask. Why do you care what happens to them?"

His silence said he hadn't thought that one through.

"I don't know," the kid said in a halting tone. "But I grow madder every time I think about them. They ruined my life. They forced my parents to hide me off world. I want them dead, Raul. I'm going there, even if I have to book passage on a public transport."

"Good luck smuggling a weapon onboard. Even the most lenient commercial liners tend to be finicky about that."

"No worries. I researched. Guns are an easy buy on Everdeen."

Nothing like a kid who had a goddamn answer for everything.

"What is your timetable, my friend? You do realize we're entering a critical phase in our expansion."

"I do. Boss, we can be in and out of there in a few hours – with a little luck. Everdeen is a seventy-nine minute jump from here. We go in with Bart, get the information from my parents, and take out those malgados before they sit down to lunch. A day trip. That's all I'm asking."

Another quality about teens that I disliked: They made everything sound so cut and dried.

"Conquillos was a day job based upon intel direct from the source, and yet we had to arrive in the middle of the night. If even one target had backed out, our objectives would have fallen short. With no intel, you expect to complete a revenge slaughter three hundred light-years away and return by dinner."

"More or less."

At least he admitted to naïve assumptions.

"And what happens when your parents, elated to learn you're alive and well, refuse to help you murder people?"

"They won't. Remember, boss. They had my arm cut off because I spoke up about The Trade. They owe me."

I didn't laugh. No sense embarrassing him.

"Ship, these people mutilated their own child. They don't strike me as the type who'd so easily regret or seek redemption. You give them more credit than they've earned."

His tone took that predictable turn where a teen digs in for the long haul, certain he'll outlast the narrow-minded adult.

"I'm going, Raul. One way or the other. Will you help me?"

The days of Ship hanging on my every word vanished without warning. Eh. The kid had to grow a mind of his own eventually.

Our forces on Bolivar were moving in on the mountain lodge. I wanted to shift my full attention there.

"I'll think about it, Ship. Make me one promise: You won't try anything foolish until I give you an answer."

"I can hold off for now. But what if you never answer?"

OK. The kid was pissing me off. I called upon Ixoca.

"Do you have any eyes on Everdeen, my friend?"

The blue pixelation formed in front of my bucket.

"I fear not, Raul," she said. "That world has no strategic value, and Aztecans are not keen to travel there."

"Few people are. The Caribs don't do much to endear themselves to off-worlders. Sexual slavery never appealed to the masses. Go figure."

I knew how this issue would ultimately resolve itself, but Ship didn't need to know. Not yet.

"Twenty days, my friend. You'll have my answer. Good?"

Ship slumped his shoulders and stared out the bubble shield. Yes, he'd grown up – from submissive teen to sulking teen.

"Fine," he said at last. "Twenty days."

"Excellent. Now, if you'll sit back and deliberate on more uplifting concepts, I need to focus on Bolivar."

"Gotcha, boss."

I watched the attack on the lodge from three angles. My partner led a wave of fighters advancing on the forward walls, which Elian was about to shred via Bart's improvised turrets. Genoa led a rear guard to cut off escape into the deep mountains. Altogether, fifty of our fighters went into this battle expecting a quick, clean wipeout.

We'd win, regardless of casualties. These mountain slugs effectively faced a UNF assault team wearing different colors. We estimated a hundred Bolivans were camped inside. If we killed everyone but Inchoa Pezos, we'd consider the mission a failure. Pezos ran that region with a grip so tight, government forces ignored it. He was one of those assholes I most hated, a real god wannabe.

Pezos rarely showed his face in public anymore, but all the mountain tribes recognized it. His followers painted the man on stone walls, usually with his arms wide open – a generous god. I saw renderings of the malgado where he stood amid a bounty of fresh fruits and vegetables. The great provider!

Yeah, no. Time for the real deal to set up shop in his territory. If we paid the locals what they deserved for working in Elian's Motif facility, they'd gladly defend us against outsiders. The Bolivans came out of the Swarm war in sorry shape because so many fell for the enemy's false god. Afterward, these people needed someone to lift them up. Pezos thought he was the man, but he didn't know the difference between lifting and punching down.

We never stretched our resources so far. Between this action, a crew holding our new production facility on Inuit Kingdom, and the teams at Conquillos, we committed a third of our army.

The first major test.

"I'm swinging about," Elian told Moon. "Final approach. Still see no missiles on the forward wall."

Moon responded with the confidence of a battlefield commander.

"We're not wrong, Elian. Soon as they catch sight of Bart, they'll fire. Genoa, sit-rep?"

"In position, boss," she said. "We'll eat them alive."

"Leave one for a snack in case we don't burn Pezos."

"On it, boss."

Goddamn, I wanted to be there. A battle like this helped to lock down the future Moon and I saw in the continuum.

After twenty years, to see it unfold in real time halfway across the sector? Maybe this was what a parent felt like watching his children from the bleachers. I could cheer, shout, or warn, but none of it would make a difference. They were on their own.

I squirmed in the bucket like a nervous nellie.

It got worse when Moon's warning came true. Six missiles launched from the forward walls, converging on Bart.

6

A T THE HEIGHT OF OUR GLORY, Moon and I could be everywhere in the nine universes at once. Or so it seemed. Nothing came close after our fall – until Ixoca's many eyes. Now, I felt the rush of a firefight on Bolivar ninety light-years away. Heard rifle blasts cut through the night. Saw a fiery flower blossom after Bart's missiles took out the lodge's forward walls. Ran into combat with my people.

Yeah, OK. It was a pale imitation. But even the sniff of what we used to have ... damn.

I marveled at the achievement. Ixoca hadn't left this planet in a hundred thousand years, but he evolved and transformed. He turned Azteca into the ultimate transmitter and receiver. He learned how to convert his three thousand terraform shafts into a network that never lost track of his heart while they spread across the galaxy.

No lifeform, organic or otherwise, spread its tentacles so damn far.

Sure. I was jealous. What of it?

I felt Elian's joy as he dodged missiles, targeted the assholes with shoulder-fired weapons, and turned the enemy into crispy critters. He loved Bart from the moment my partner and I landed in town. Now he flew her like the UNF-trained pilot he never became.

49

He handled my beautiful sedan with the expertise of a craftsman who knew every inch of her systems, but he seasoned the effort with the relish of a stone cold killer. Elian was everything I embodied in my rampaging early years. Full ahead, kill what's in front of me, count the bodies later.

As the forward walls collapsed, he aimed the big guns at the manor house. He focused on the fools retreating inside, as if they'd have a fighting chance. Were they preparing to surround Pezos for a final stand?

Just before Elian strafed the malgados, he shouted in my voice:

"Sleep well, my friends!"

He spent months refining that impression. He found a happy medium between the dulcet tones of a suave salesman and the wisdom of an elder who'd knocked around the universes for a bit.

When I asked him once about impersonating me, he wasn't embarrassed in the slightest.

"Nothing but glitter, boss. It's my little tribute for all you've done."

I hoped to hear that 'tribute' for years to come but feared its owner would flame out much too soon. Humans like him died young, and he lacked the benefit of regeneration. To make matters extra dicey, Elian would draw a huge target on his back after his Motif empire exploded. Competitors were inevitable.

After my partner led his squad into the burning lodge, Moon ordered Elian to pull back.

"We'll take it from here. Return to the facility."

"Will do, boss. I'll expect a pop-in soon as you finish cleanup."

Pop-in. That's how our lieutenants referred to our vocal intrusion inside their minds. It was a convenient tool for Moon and me, but we had the advantage of living with our *D'ru-shayas* for centuries.

I stayed clear while they concentrated on the fight. Genoa's team made target practice out of the retreating enemy. She was more clinical in a fight than Elian. She was poised with a rifle, made every shot count, and quickly earned the veterans' respect. I gave her better odds at longevity.

Victory was never in question, only the matter of finding Pezos. The search took Moon and his team into tunnels beneath the lodge.

That's where they surrounded the old slug an hour after the fires petered out. Pezos hunkered down in a cavern behind a thick metal door he foolishly expected to keep him safe. Four of his mindless minions and two surviving sons – apparently, he started the night with five children – formed a pointless phalanx around him.

Moon surprised me. He didn't explode their hearts with a thought or order his team to rush in and gun them down. My partner actually toyed with the bastards. A new Moon for a new era!

"We warned you, Pezos," he shouted from the cavern's outer chamber. "We promised to burn it all to the ground. There's nothing left. Stop hiding behind your men."

He didn't, but our defeated enemy had one last pitiful play.

"You win, Black Star. But you are wrong to say we have nothing left. I have a stockpile of fascia-cut blood gems. They are pure, untraceable. They can earn seventy, eighty million. Allow me to leave with my sons, and half the treasure is yours."

"Only half? Where's the stash, Pezos?"

"No. You must agree to my terms."

Moon sighed. His learning curve toward patience remained long.

I took this as a good opportunity to intervene.

"A stockpile of gems would help purchase a fleet," I said.

"Agreed, but you don't expect me to negotiate with this idiot."

"No. Not at all, my friend. Here's an idea."

Moon found my plan doable and fun (since he was in the toying frame of mind).

"Here's how it's going to work," Moon shouted. "Send out your sons unarmed. If the gems are real, they know where to find them. They'll point the way. When Black Star controls the entire stash, we'll let you leave with the shirts on your back. You won't get a better offer."

All things considered, it was a fair deal.

A man of Pezos' background would take it. He didn't mind humbling himself if it meant he could someday scheme to reclaim his lost kingdom and exact revenge.

After a long, awkward silence, the asshole conceded.

"Truba and Hento are coming out. They are unarmed. They will lead you to the gems."

This fella was pitiful. He and his father had squeezed that entire mountain region for half a century. It wasn't listed as a sovereign state on any map, but it might as well have been. If this king of the hills had a spine, he would've walked out ahead of his boys.

I'd seen this sad tale play out many times. Pezos kept alive a long tradition among wannabe gods: *Me first and last, above all others.*

The sons did not engender pity. They wore beards capable of nesting the babies of many diminutive species. One had a large vertical scar beneath his left eye.

I suspected some serious inbreeding.

Moon was direct.

"Where is it? Be specific."

Truba and Hento didn't seem to know who should speak first. Mr. Scar deferred to his brother by pointing at Moon.

"The gems are close. They are hidden in the mountains."

Moon chuckled, but it came out like a grunt.

"Bullshit. If they exist at all, they'd be kept on the property in a secure location. This cavern seems like a perfect place."

"No. Y-you will ... you must follow us. We will take you there."

Moon retrieved a cigar. I was surprised he waited so long.

"*We?* That don't work for us. *You.* Which one are you?"

"Truba."

Moon addressed his squad. "So, Truba is going to take us to the gems. Hento will fall to his knees and remain there until we find the stash. Truba, you've got five minutes at most because those gems are nearby. What'll it be?"

"Five minutes? No. That's not enough."

"Sure it is. Your loving father intends to split us up. Give himself the best chance to slink out of here. A hidden door? A passage we don't know about? Yeah. I see it in your eyes. Now. Take us to the gems, Truba, or this is where your bones will lie to the end of recorded time ... something I'm familiar with."

Oh, the relish Moon put into this gamesmanship. He added an exciting new oratory skillset.

Very proud of my partner.

Truba's eyes gave up the ghost. Did Moon see it, too?

Still, the jackass told his brother to take a knee, and Truba started toward Moon. This fella did not know how to improvise.

"It is through there," Truba said, pointing to the corridor Moon's team arrived through. "Follow me."

Moon slipped aside. I wanted to see his reaction. Was he smirking?

"Troll, Happy, go with him." Two of his squad escorted Truba, while Moon and three others remained. He watched until the gem-seekers rounded a bend.

"OK, Pezos. We're split up now. There's four of us out here against five of you in there. If you like your odds, feel free to play Fast-Gun Jose." He stared down at Hento. "For the record, I think your boy's about to piss his pants."

"No," Pezos said. "You made a deal. The gems for our lives."

"Except you're bluffing."

"You are wrong. The gems are real. They will make you very wealthy. Please. You have my word."

"Not talking about the gems, Pezos. I meant their location. You were on the run. We had you beat. A desperate man salvages what he can. You're carrying those gems. Now, as I see it, you got two choices. Shoot your way out or hand them over. What'll it be?"

Moon's soldiers aimed chest-high, ready for the onslaught. Moon slung his own rifle over his shoulder. Interesting.

Would Pezos send his guardians to die? Would they commit suicide in his name?

My partner was experiencing the thrill of a tactic he long thought dull and excessive. Yes, my friend, it was more than OK to take your time killing a foe.

His patience was rewarded moments later when Pezos said:

"We're coming out unarmed. I have the gems."

Moon whispered to his team: "Triggers."

Four men emerged with hands held high. They were searched and ordered to their knees.

Pezos followed.

His beard was silver but not sufficiently large enough for nesting. His unibrow reminded me of Lumen.

"The gems?" Moon asked.

Pezos removed a satchel from his back and tossed it forward.

"Wait." Moon scanned it for explosives. "Good. Pezos, on your knees." Moon opened the satchel.

Holy. Shit.

The gems resembled rain drops with a red tint. I'd seen this effect during the monsoon season on the Naugista Plateau. Pezos wasn't exaggerating. Hell, he might have undervalued these cuts.

"Assuming they aren't brilliant fakes, my friend, I think we just purchased a half-dozen spaceworthy Barts."

He chuckled. "How about three Barts and a transport?"

"Or that. They'll go along nicely with our new Scramjet."

This conversation never left the inside of our minds, so no one gazed at Moon in confusion.

"Finish your business, my friend. Perhaps we'll discuss it over drinks tonight. Yes?"

"See you then, partner."

He grabbed Pezos by the collar and lifted him with one hand until the old bastard met him eye to eye.

"You done good, Pezos. You bought your ticket to freedom. Well, almost bought. There's one last thing I need from you."

Oh, I didn't see this epilogue coming.

"What more can I give?" Pezos had to know he was out of time.

"Say it, Pezos: Black Star runs these mountains now."

I thought the malgado might spit on my partner instead.

He complied, word for word. But that wasn't good enough.

"Black Star will offer a job to everyone," Moon added. "Black Star will treat all Bolivans fairly."

Pezos stammered through the words until Moon made sure he got them right. Now, I understood. Moon was recording it! Preparing it for playback, just like Ixoca did when he showed us the crash of Orpheus. We'd guarantee the mountain folk that Pezos was gone for good.

"Last words, Pezos: No one loyal to me will ever walk these lands again. If they do, you must shoot them on sight."

Pezos refused, of course. It did seem a bit extreme.

"Why? You won. Isn't that enough?"

"Say the words or I shoot your son in the head."

Moon remembered the classic strategy: Loved ones in peril. Pezos gave in. Moon made him repeat the lines until they sounded genuine.

"Perfect. Thank you for all your help. And the gems."

"You promised to let us leav ..."

Pezos never said another word. His eyes rolled back in his head, and blood poured from his nose. When Moon let go, Pezos fell like a puppet without a handler.

My partner turned to his soldiers.

"Kill these cunts."

Hento and the four guardians took their laser bolts like men. No pouting or begging.

Moon grabbed the satchel.

"What did you think?" He asked me.

"A beautiful mix of brute force, intimidation, and verbal misdirection. The recording? A stroke of brilliance. That'll help enormously with public relations. And the gems are quite a lovely bonus, my friend."

"Have to admit: It feels good. Like the old days."

"Any thoughts about the other son?"

They entered the corridor not far behind the misguided Pezos heir. Moon laughed.

"We'll escort him to the surface. I want him to see what's left of his family's empire. Then I'll crush his throat."

"Gorgeous. I'd say this has been our most fruitful day. Expanding a business is fun."

"It is, partner."

The sun had barely risen on our great enterprise. So many wonderful challenges ahead.

Ixoca waited until the Bolivan adventure concluded before he reappeared inside the driver's bucket.

"I have been monitoring Martin Jimenez while your eye shifted across the stars."

"Oh, yes? Has he followed through?"

"He submitted his resignation to Parliament. He beat your deadline by thirty-six seconds."

Good. One less nuisance.

"You'll do your best to keep him in line, my friend?"

"He'll follow the path. I expect him to begin his machinations within days."

"No doubt. Watch him carefully, Ixoca. I prefer to filter these eyes toward other fronts. We'll be expanding operations on two planets, and I'm targeting two more within the month. I'll need to see how the Prez responds and search for new additions to our interstellar fleet. I juggle many plates, my friend."

Ixoca pressed his pixelated fingers together as if praying.

"I'd so hate for you to encounter a setback. I'll make sure you have everything in place before I ask my favor."

The favor.

Moon and I always knew Ixoca would want something huge in return for his gifts. Yet the Jewel remained vague on that front. *The favor*, he called it. When we pressed Ixoca for details, he said only that his request would represent "fair compensation." Afterwards, he insisted, we would decouple and go our separate ways.

Eh. If history taught anything, folks who made deals with the gods played a game of the highest risk-reward.

Fortunately, we weren't a pair of schmucks. Or worse, humans. If Ixoca had sold us a bill of goods, we knew a few tricks of the trade.

"Now, if you'll excuse me, Ixoca, I'd like to celebrate a bountiful pair of victories with my young apprentice."

"Fair enough, Royal. Until next time."

I popped into Ship's mind.

"Good news, my friend. All our objectives at Conquillos and the Matzenor Prefecture on Bolivar have been achieved."

"That's the best news, boss. Did we lose anyone on Bolivar?"

"No, although our perfect streak is certain to end soon. Many obstacles lie ahead. Ship, we have two hours to Desperido. I thought you might fill some of that time by regaling me with stories."

He shot me a perplexed glance through the bubble shield.

"About what, boss?"

"Everdeen. You're eager to return there and kill everyone who betrayed you. Yes? I thought perhaps you might tell me about the place. I ignored it during my travels."

"Sure. Uh. Does that mean I have your blessing to ...?"

"Keep your excitement tucked in your pants, my friend. Tell me of your home world. It's a limited-time offer."

I didn't actually want to know anything about that miserable planet, but if Ship talked long enough, he might reconsider.

For the next hour, he dragged out stories from his childhood, few of any intrigue. In the meantime, I shifted my many eyes across the stars and dreamed of the coming interstellar storm.

I soon learned trouble was already brewing close to home, right under my goddamn nose.

7

DESPERIDO CONTROL LOWERED the outer defense shield as we approached from the west. From this position, visitors saw a weary desert town with fifty dust-covered heaps. We created this mirage through a projection; the cloak we nicknamed the oasis dome fooled surveillance drones and satellites. We built a new reality beneath it.

Twelve modules, each twenty meters diameter, surrounded the eastern edge of town. We equipped them with hydrogardens, water reclamation systems, and individual living pods that were downright luxurious compared to the bunker network. Some of our three hundred recruits brought vehicles that they donated to our cause. Desperido became more active above ground than below.

We gave our soldiers the best resources for two practical reasons. One, they stood ready to fight and die. Two, if gods couldn't provide acceptable housing, why would anyone sacrifice for the cheap sons of bitches?

The original militia had a choice to either turn in their weapons and resume the old ways down below or fall under Bett's command in the new army and move into a module. Moon and I thought most would choose the latter. However, only a handful met the challenge of joining what Bett called 'proper fucking soldiery.' Truth be told, they weren't physically suited to Bett's regimen.

Chief among them: Saul.

One of our earliest members to the table of trust, Saul gave it a go. After three days of Bett's training routines, he admitted the obvious. He wasn't a soldier. However, he understood people. Saul looked into one's eyes and saw the truth with little or no backstory.

His temperament and erudition suited him as the man in the middle.

Caretaker of Desperido. Liaison between contractors and soldiers. A many for every season. An administrator I no longer wished to be.

Mayor.

Our first and likely last, given the town's precarious state.

Saul greeted Ship and me with a cordial smile after I parked Red Dust amongst our other overland chasers. He carried the ubiquitous tablet he preferred to a pom.

"Pleasant journey, Raul?"

"I was not disappointed, my friend."

These days, Saul dressed sharply enough to warrant respect at a town confab but not so urbane as to seem like an interloper. He wore dark glasses and a wide-brimmed woven hat outside; the sun took its toll after years of subterranean life. He wasn't the only longtime contractor to fit that bill.

Saul nodded toward Ship.

"And what of your young protégé?"

The kid beamed.

"Killed one. Cremated six."

"You're making a name for yourself. Congratulations."

They shook hands. The kid displayed a firm grip; Bett taught him better than I the value of such a thing.

"Thanks, Mayor. I'm building my rep, one mission at a time. Someday, I'll command my own unit. You'll see."

Oh, please. I didn't dispute that Ship might round into a decent leader. If he survived that long. I hated the notion that he intended to get there through a resume built on murder. Too many humans thought the ability to take out other assholes imbued them with a special sauce. *Fear me, respect me, for I have slaughtered!*

Yeah, no.

Murder (the cold-blooded variety) suited humans who embraced it as a function of nature. A preordained facet of life. Those who turned to murder because of ambition, passion, or self-righteousness (the majority) were inevitably destroyed by it.

Guilt, remorse, depression, psychotic breaks. These things ate at an amateur killer's inner world. Reduced them to flaky shells not worth the air they consumed.

Sure. OK. Ship had slaughtered a few guys, set corpses ablaze, and come out the other end smiling. That hardly guaranteed his destiny as a remorse-free assassin capable of leading other men down the same path. Such finesse required a special touch reserved to a limited few like myself.

"Ship, my friend, please report in with Commander Ortiz. We'll speak again later on those personal matters."

The kid almost forgot his place. Though he remained at the trusted table, Ship wore the same desert camouflage as every man and woman in our army. He cleared his activities through Bett and the sergeant assigned to his module.

Ship snapped his feet together and saluted.

"Yes, boss. Right away. And ... thank you for listening, boss."

After the kid left hearing range, Saul said:

"Should I ask?"

"He has revenge on his mind, my friend. I blame myself. I kept a promise to Lumen, which goes to prove I'm fallible."

"Or honorable, depending upon one's point of view."

Saul defaulted to the positive by instinct.

"You give me too much credit, Saul."

I watched Ship disappear into Mod 1, where Bett lived. Several of her units drilled toward the south perimeter. Most of our vets were in their forties or fifties and still working toward peak fighting condition. Many arrived out of shape, physically and emotionally. These particular units had yet to be used in the field. I employed perhaps the oldest army in history; other than Ship and Elian, the youngest fighter was thirty-five.

History would never claim our criminal empire lacked experience.

"Now, Saul. What's bothering you?"

He stifled a laugh. "How did you know?"

"You made a point of waiting in my spot. You wanted to grab my attention before anyone else."

"That transparent, am I?"

We stopped outside the cantina, nodding as soldiers passed nearby.

"Tell me."

"We have a growing problem, Raul. I fear it is about to escalate."

Lovely.

"Go on, my friend."

"Soldiers are abusing the care workers. At times, the assaults have been violent. I received five reports in the past six days."

"Be more specific. Define *violent.*"

Understandably, Saul had too much self-respect to describe the violations in graphic detail. He showed me an image of Enid, the youngest care worker and someone Moon visited in the early days. Her right eye was surrounded by an island of purple, and her lip was cut.

"Is it the same man?"

"No, Raul. There's no pattern. More often, they cross the line between consensual intercourse and rape. The women won't officially name the violators. They're afraid of reprisals. And frankly, boss, some have no other skills."

"OK. So, they're afraid we'll send them north."

Saul nodded. "Since you instituted the policy requiring everyone to contribute or else ..."

"Which I don't regret. You told me yourself labor efficiency had increased by forty percent. Why haven't you brought this problem to the table?"

"Commander Ortiz would say I was exaggerating, that the incidents were isolated. She and lieutenants Tolan and Sisal are very protective of their people."

"They feel betrayed by this planet and its leaders. Their wounds are binding and run deep."

Saul rolled his eyes. Yes, it was a lousy excuse but also true.

"Everyone in Desperido feels cast off in some way. If anything, it should be a unifying factor."

"Do you suggest I call together all nine hundred residents for a session of spiritual healing, my friend?"

He didn't appreciate my snark. Few ever did.

"Please don't be dismissive, Raul. This town is divided into two populations: Military and civilian. The latter have noticed the luxuriant conditions provided to the former."

The hair on my back would've stood if I had any.

"They're unsatisfied? Everyone was offered the chance to join."

"That's not the word I'd use. *Forgotten*. They feel forgotten since your attention turned to matters far beyond Desperido."

"Building a future, you mean? Saul, our contractors have made more money in the past six months than the previous six years. It's theirs to spend if they want to upgrade their bunkers. Obviously, we don't want animosity, but I fail to see the depth of the problem. Why don't you and I sit down with Stopper, Tracer, and Inky? We can lay out new ground rules for use of the care workers."

He waved me inside the cantina.

"There's something you need to see, boss."

We entered without fanfare to a crowded cantina. Every table and most bar stools were occupied, a common occurrence these days.

The staff, compromised of five contractors who took over after Lumen's departure, worked as an experienced team.

"Business booms, my friend. What should disturb me?"

"I'm amazed you don't see it. Not one table is integrated. If not for the barkeeps, there'd be no interaction between the soldiers and the civilians."

He was right. Desert camouflage appeared in islands surrounded by the diaspora of our misbegotten individualists.

"To be fair, Saul, the contractors weren't the most social creatures when I first arrived. The veterans came here to fight for something bigger than themselves. The civilians ran away, for the most part. I don't mean to offend."

"None taken. Boss, you're right about the differences. And we've rarely had trouble in here. But this is the town's one common area. The atmosphere is different in the bunkers. There's a growing chorus demanding action to protect the care workers. And that's just a start."

"How so?"

"Many advocate a work stoppage."

Great. I looked away for a few weeks, and the humans made a mess of things. What should I have expected?

"Not likely to happen, Saul. Half their livelihoods are tied to Motif. Does Elian know?"

"His eyes are focused on expansion. He moved his top lieutenants to operations on Inuit and Bolivar."

"Who's minding the store here?"

"Many chefs run that kitchen now. Much like in here."

"But profits are still on the upswing?"

His sigh suggested a nudge of impatience at my attitude.

"They are, boss. For now."

I led Saul into the back office and closed the door.

"Saul, these problems did not gather moss overnight. Why am I only now learning of them?"

"Raul, you entrusted me as the town's administrator. You and Ilan gave me full authority to oversee internal operations and handle conflict management to the best of my ability."

"Yes, those were the terms. Thank you for restating them."

That wasn't fair of me, but this whole matter had dampened my joy following a hard day's work.

"Raul, if I might be blunt?"

"I've never encouraged you otherwise, my friend."

He tucked away his tablet.

"You and Ilan are our generals. Regardless of the authority you hand to me or Commander Ortiz, the ultimate responsibility for this town and its people remains firmly yours. I understand delegating responsibility, but that can lead to involuntary neglect. I would not have come to you with this problem if I believed a resolution was within my power to achieve."

I couldn't get angry at Saul. Everything he said felt purposeful and well considered. I appreciated a man of linguistic integrity.

"I've no doubt you tried your best, Saul. I could rattle off excuses, of course. The many eyes of Ixoca are a constant distraction. Our missions require extensive planning. Buying equipment for the modules on the night market is tedious. Indoctrinating the recruits is time-consuming. Converting syneth reserves to hydrogarden accelerants is physically taxing. It's quite a checklist."

I left several items off, but he got the point.

"Your plate is full, Raul. Understood. Which is why I avoided a confrontation. Only after Commander Ortiz briefed us upon her return and we learned of the success on Bolivar, did I decide to inject this matter into your affairs. I thought perhaps you'd have a brief interlude."

"In other words, catch the boss when he's in a good mood."

We shared a comfortable smile.

"Something like that," he said.

"No, Saul. You're right. We should seal the rift before it grows. I have a strategy in mind, but I'll need your help. Arrange a meeting with the abused care workers. Leave the rest to me. Good?"

I saw suspicion in his eyes.

"Yes. One request: I'd like to be there also. I'll risk losing credibility otherwise."

"Certainly."

There it was. In the wake of our most significant victories to date, I was forced to settle a human relations matter. Serious, for certain, but very much ... human.

The most nitpicky might blame me for the conflict given that Desperido had no written system of justice, let alone guidelines for how to treat the neighbors. Frankly, the town successfully dealt with its few extremists and malingerers over the decades. However, those punishments exceeded what Saul was willing to dispense. I did not have the same qualms.

An hour later, I waited inside the phasic trauma medpod, which we extended to include invasive triage tools. We used it twice on recent missions for life-threatening injuries. Never ceased to amaze me what wonders could be purchased on the night market.

Six care workers entered with Saul. I never spent time with them – only one might have qualified as my type – but I remembered their names. Enid, Malva, Diego, Hortense, Celia, and Brie. Enid was twenty-six, Malva forty-seven, the rest in between. They possessed a certain beauty, if not slightly artificial. No enhancements (not even wigs), just good skin and bright eyes. For now. Time would not serve them well.

"Please, my friends, have a seat."

Per our agreement, Saul remained at the door while I sat in front of the semi-circle like a group counselor.

"Mayor Saul says you have been grossly mistreated. I am outraged. I have expressed my displeasure at the scope of this issue and how it has been allowed to persist for so long. My goal today is to seek a resolution through punishment and proper compensation."

Yes, I picked up a few tricks watching politicians through Ixoca's eyes. The Prez in particular. I tossed Saul under the train, but he knew my verbal tactics. He'd get over it.

"Enid." I addressed the young woman. "Your eye is looking better."

She lifted a hand toward it reflexively.

"Thank you, boss. The phasics are miraculous."

"Hmm. They are indeed. Have you returned to work since the incident, Enid?"

She tightened her arms against her chest.

"Not yet, boss."

"How much longer will you need?"

"Three days. Maybe four."

"Good." I shifted my focus to the others. "How about the rest of you? Is anyone currently unable to work?"

Three raised their hands.

"Tell me, Diego. Why?"

Eye contact was not his thing today. The most pivotal tool for a care worker, and he couldn't deliver.

"I don't feel safe, boss."

"Who else feels the same?"

All raised a hand.

Huh. I wasn't a therapist and damn well had no patience for molly-coddling. Best to lay out the stakes first.

"As you know, the primary rule of Desperido is clear. Everyone must contribute. So, what can I do to ensure you return to the job and avoid the alleged work stoppage your neighbors propose?"

They glanced at each other and Saul.

"You're free to speak your mind, people. I seek resolution."

Malva, the oldest, found some courage.

"Banishment, boss. Everyone who has hurt us needs to be sent into the desert without water or supplies."

"Ah, the old ways. I could, assuming we first give the accused a chance to defend themselves. That might be long and messy and further split this town. In addition, the soldiers know survival skills. It's likely they'll outlast a desert sentence."

"They crossed the line," said Celia, a thirtysomething brunette with a birth mark near her dimple. "Some of these soldiers are animals. The things they force us to do are …"

When she choked up, Diego wrapped an arm around her.

"Boss, all we ask is justice," he said. "We dealt with abusers long before these veterans arrived. Our jobs are not easy, but all we want is to give pleasure to people in need of it. Celia's right. Some are unstable. I had a client last week who called me by the name of his ex-boyfriend. He threatened to cut me to shreds because I ruined his life. I thought I was going to die."

Diego kept his body finely honed. Most likely, he enacted some justice in the moment.

"Marva votes for the desert. What about you, Diego?"

"It's not enough to send these malgados away. The others will just come around and do the same things."

I nodded. This guy understood human behavior.

"Correct. You'll almost certainly face reprisals."

"That's why we need a law. Something simple, boss. We deserve respect. We give more of ourselves than anyone else in this town."

"That can be arranged. But what of the guilty?"

"Make an example, boss. I don't care how, but it should be public. That's how things used to be done. Out on the central avenue."

Marva, Celia, and Hortense nodded firm agreement.

"Enid, what would you say to the idea of banning the army from access to your services?"

The very notion struck fear into her big blue eyes.

"I … I don't know. They pay very well, boss."

"I see. Before the recruits arrived, did you have empty days on your calendar?" She nodded. "And now?"

"When I was working? Six or seven clients a day."

The others concurred with those gratifying statistics. I removed the ban from my options.

"And you will again, Enid. But this time, you will be treated with respect and dignity."

"Thank you, boss."

"Don't thank me yet. There's something each of you must do."

8

MOON AND I WEREN'T BUILDERS, and we damn well had no interest in city planning. That changed when Stopper, Tracer, and Inky reached out to their mates and recruited the foundation to our army. Pup tents, open fires, and squatting in the desert weren't acceptable conditions for a fighting force, so we scrambled to remake Desperido.

Between the night market and legitimate supplies via road train, we burned through close to a million UCVs and stockpiled enough equipment for the next three modules. Construction took most of our days for the first several weeks of expansion and amounted to more physical labor than either of us had undertaken ... ever.

To clarify a point: It was the most *tedious* labor. We worked much harder long ago slaughtering immortal opponents in a place called the Corral, and we relentlessly pursued the Creators across five light-years for almost a century before wiping them out. But those were labors of love.

Here, we built a luxurious add-on knowing full well it would be abandoned within the year. A desert oasis soon to be hidden beneath a stain of red dust.

We concluded that the sacrifice (and short-term financial loss) amounted to a worthy investment. The rent-free living conditions intoxicated recruits and made them malleable to indoctrination.

Oh, sure, they came to us already disaffected and ready to lash out at convenient targets. However, the royal treatment told them we were serious. Early counseling by their military leaders and a demonstration of our special talents placated all but a handful of vets.

The few who refused to commit were sent away, their memories wiped. Ixoca's terraform matrix gave us the ability to reassemble human minds. We promised Bett not to harm anyone who rebuffed us, but we couldn't guarantee the wipe would leave all brain functions untouched. We dropped them off at a public transit station outside Machado, with a few UCVs on hand.

The other ninety-five percent signed a binding contract. They gave their lives to us. Yes, we guaranteed they'd play a role in silencing the powers who wished to betray Azteca. Beyond that, however, they vowed loyalty to us and our interstellar agenda.

We promised them the stars and wealth beyond measure. (OK, so the last bit might have been an exaggeration.)

We promised them freedom from the rule of law and an ability to fight all comers by any means necessary. (So long as they followed *our* particular set of laws.)

We promised to provide for the families they might have left behind. A majority had kids but didn't fit into the traditional social structure. Like Bett, they never truly escaped the war. (Moon and I had no plan for how to do this, nor did we consider it a priority. Hence, we lied. Or perhaps we'd reach a solution down the road. Eh.)

All they had to do? Follow orders without question.

Ixoca expressed envy at how quickly we seduced and mollified these veterans to our unique perspective. While I would've liked to take full credit – my linguistic mastery, my dulcet tones, my patronizing platitudes – the truth was more complex. I credited The Wave.

"Think of a grand dinner table," I explained to Ixoca during our many late-night musings. "Beautiful place settings. A fine centerpiece, all sitting atop a white cloth. Then along comes a trickster. He grabs hold of the cloth and yanks it from the table in one deft move.

"Glasses, plates, silverware, centerpiece. They move, but only for a split second, and remain in place. However, an observer cannot help but view the table in a different light. Gone is the artifice which hid all the minor imperfections of the tabletop. They see it as if for the first time.

"This, my friend, is what happened twenty years ago. The Wave allowed humans to see truths long hidden behind a white cloth. Concepts they would have struggled to accept before, instantly became credible. All they needed was a nudge. Something new to believe in. That would be Moon and I."

Ixoca questioned my assertion.

"Is it you they follow, or the ideals of separation from society? An unfettered existence where savagery is accepted practice? Have there not always been small segments of humanity willing to divorce themselves from the rigors of civilization?"

I chuckled like the sixteen-year-old boy who committed his first murder on Hokkaido.

"Of course. I was an early adopter, my friend. I grew up in a city of twenty million, yet I spent more time hiding in the shadows than basking in the sunlight. It was the only way to survive. I was always afraid of being caught. These fighters have no such concern. The civilized will become the outsiders."

"And what of Black Star?"

"We're the truth. We're what's left behind when the tablecloth is yanked away."

Ixoca admired my metaphor though he expressed reservations about my vision. He thought Black Star would generate more than enough enemies to wipe us out within a few years.

"Humans, for all their flaws, insist upon order. They will fight any force bent on disrupting that order, Royal."

"They're predictable. Yes. But we won't be an army with a uniform and a flag. We'll be so endemic on so many worlds, we'll become a disease they can't eradicate. If they want us gone, they'd best get to work. Fast."

I wasn't worried. The Collectorate embodied the principles of order in its Constitution, but it lacked the will to underline those words. One particle missile from a UNF warship would fry this town and everything within twenty kilometers.

They did not have the will.

I preached this message to my fighters. Loud enough. Long enough. Often enough.

On the whole, Moon and I offered a square deal, although we expected a few outliers to lose their cognitive shit along the way. We wanted men and women who compartmentalized their killings rather than dwell on moral implications. Nothing good would come of such a time-wasting venture.

We thought camaraderie, drinks, and a small group of care workers would top off the experience. In retrospect, we might've been a tad too optimistic. Or downright naïve.

Either way, the matter had to be put to rest, and the growing rift in Desperido closed. I initiated my plan at sunset.

Bett, Saul, and Moon each thought my proposed tactics carried a risk but supported the larger goal. Worst case, I told them: "Our army will suffer one casualty, and we'll take a second crack tomorrow."

I chose the most public location: Central avenue. Each night, after the sun vanished and the town settled into muted merriment, dozens of soldiers convened on the avenue roughly where the tumblers made their weekly stops. Some dragged chairs, others brought pillows or blankets, and most came equipped with alcohol. The smell of cigars and the sweet leaf from digipipes dominated the setting.

They surrounded a portable glow lamp and proceeded to tell their stories. Most focused on the Swarm war and its aftermath. Others on the systemic corruption that betrayed them. Some became emotional, unveiling their deepest secrets. The Circle, as it became known, turned into a support group. They strengthened each other through shared pain, a process Bett and I agreed would serve them well.

Only a week earlier, Ship found the courage to speak before the group and discuss his life on Azteca. He talked of what it meant to finally be accepted despite his Carib birth.

The fighters came here to heal, but only the fighters. That was about to change.

I approached the Circle but lingered in the shadows. Listening, observing. I counted about seventy fighters, including a handful who Bett encouraged to attend without saying why. My eyes fell upon the one who would soon play a critical role.

"Are you ready?" I asked Saul without opening my lips.

He waited in a cube with the six care workers and heard my voice echo in his mind.

"We're good here, boss."

"Everyone understands their roles and my cues?"

"They do."

The six squirmed with obvious anxiety, especially the designated speakers, but their eyes were brighter, more hopeful.

"They'll see it through?"

"We've talked at length, Raul. They're nervous but also quite brave. They see the wisdom in your plan."

"Good. Bring them out in ten minutes."

I saw Bett in the lamplight, smoking a cheroot and laughing at the story her oldest fighter told. She didn't see me but knew I was here. We had discussed my plan at length. It was a robust session where she forced me to adapt to her many concerns, all valid. This had to proceed with care, or we risked breaking the bonds so delicately forged.

Moon watched through my eyes en route from Bolivar. I asked him to bring Bart out of the wormhole a few kilometers south of town so the aperture's thunder wouldn't disrupt the moment.

Sgt. Ezra "Glue" Montero continued his tale of escapades during UNF basic training to a rapt audience.

"Then the kid looks at me with a straight face and says, 'Colonel, my rifle jammed three times today and Sgt. Willhouser refused to assign me a new one.'"

Glue pointed to the few who laughed out loud.

"Yeah, yeah. You know where this story is headed. Anyway, I put my hands on my hips and faked total outrage. The kid must've thought I'd bring the hammer down on Sgt. Willhouser. Instead, I stared at his scrawny ass and said, '1st Mate Indowi, what was the nature of today's drill?' To which he quickly replied, 'Friend vs. foe.' I nodded and then replied, 'Correct.'" A few more knowing laughs ensued. "I reminded him that the rifles were programmed to fire only upon the transponder beacons of the simulated enemy."

A fighter with a small cigar tucked between his teeth said:

"What was his defense?"

"Hah. He didn't have one. When I explained that he tried to kill his own people three times, Indowi said, 'But Colonel, you never know. They could've been double agents.'"

Raucous laughter ensued. I chuckled along with the crowd. It was a fun story, if not apocryphal. Glue was a UNF Colonel who never saw combat. He supervised at bases like Conquillos on three different planets. These trifling tales were likely his most interesting.

Now he was the sergeant in charge of Mod 8. He saw his first live fire a month ago when we cleared out territory on Inuit Kingdom and ran into some unexpected pushback. He returned from that rotation a week ago and declared, "I haven't felt that alive since my first fuck."

Glue lacked the agility I expected in my fighters, but we'd send him into the field a few more times. He earned that much.

After he finished his tale, I sauntered ahead and into the lamp's glow. Tradition called for the speaker to take a drink and pass along the ceremonial flask to the next. Glue started toward an apparent volunteer, but I interrupted.

"If it's OK, my friend," I told the soldier, "I have a few words to say." As if he would object? Glue handed me the flask, which I sipped before staring out at the fighters.

"It occurred to me that I never stood before you in this context."

I had shared many parts of my backstory with them during indoctrination, and rarely the same tale twice. Except for the most titillating details their minds weren't yet prepared to handle, they learned enough to know I never played by the rules.

"I must warn you right off: I lack Glue's sense of humor. Perhaps when I'm his age in ... oh ... twenty or thirty years ..."

The laughter returned following my well-timed zinger.

"But seriously, age and wisdom tend to bundle well. We're fortunate to have someone of Glue's experience. Now, you're wondering why I chose tonight to enter the Circle. It's complicated, my friends. However, certain concerns have arisen that I believe need to be addressed. Before we do, I'd like to share a piece of my life as a soldier. It offers an important lesson that I hope will guide us in our future conquests."

They hung on my every word, of course. But first, I popped inside Bett's mind.

"The others will be joining us soon?"

"Sure will, boss. I ordered a few of my sergeants to spread the word. Circle should be filling out."

"Thank you, Stopper."

Ixoca intervened, this time as the blue female.

"Take care, Raul. Both our goals could suffer a setback if you do not handle this well."

I imagined rolling my eyes.

"Point taken. Again."

The Jewel had a tendency to reemphasize principles I understood the first time. I was not an idiot. To my audience, I said:

75

"All of you know I was born immortal. You also know I don't live with the Aeternans because I share nothing else in common with them. They claim to be a huge family, but they don't follow my view of the universe. If I sat down to a meal with them, one of two things would happen. I'd piss them off and they'd show me the door. Or I'd be the one mysterious relative who never says a word while everyone else chatters like nattering nabobs. Nothing in common.

"There was a time long ago when I *did* have such a family. We were drawn together in blood and sacrifice. We fought the Swarm before anyone did in Alpha Universe."

I waited for the nods of recognition. Were they putting the pieces together to a secret I had yet to divulge?

"I fought in a unit of a great army called the Twenty Talons. We battled their forces in Beta Universe. It was a futile war. The combat was conducted between soldiers wearing almost impenetrable, organic body armor. The brutality exceeded anything experienced on this side of the divide. Savagery beyond description.

"And yet, it was beautiful. It was perfect. It was endless. There was freedom in the hopelessness. Why, you ask? Because death was always thick in the air. Because we expected to die on the battlefield. Because we endured together as one mind bent on defying the inevitable.

"I died many times, but my genetic design refused to surrender. This meant I outlived most of my mortal brothers and sisters. I rose through the ranks by default. But the title mattered less than the respect and love we felt for each other. We were ... *one*. Always."

I gave them a moment to reflect upon their own histories. Most were Hornet pilots who launched from UNF warships intent on breaking through largely impregnable Swarm cruiser shields called the Crust. Tiny vessels – mere gnats to the enemy – created a magnetic web to disrupt the Crust and its millions of nanodrones.

"The enemy?" I continued. "We showed zero mercy. But they never relented. Never retreated. And damn well never surrendered.

76

They fought for a false god. We fought for each other. Family. One.

"And then, an opportunity to change fate fell into our laps after six years. We crossed the divide. Yes, I belonged to that now-legendary group who first arrived on Hokkaido, who manned the Scylla before she became famous. Yes, you know some of the names of that crew. One is President of the Collectorate. One is High Admiral. The others staked their claims through many trials. Some fell, but most now live happily in Alpha.

"You may ask: Raul, why aren't you mentioned among those legends? I'll tell you true: Because I broke the bond of our family. I betrayed them in a selfish, psychotic act. They cast me aside, a punishment I deserved. Since then, I have journeyed alone but for Ilan. We were all the family we needed.

"Now we have more. We have you. Three hundred brothers and sisters who refuse to play by the rules. Three hundred who can exist in a world where death is in the air. Who will live and die as one."

That drew a strong round of applause, as well it should have. They thought I was here to provide inspiration.

They thought wrong.

"And yet, we are not whole. We are not one. Not yet."

My eyes turned to the latest arrivals, whose faces now glowed in the lamp light.

Time for the main event.

9

BART APPROACHED FROM THE SOUTH, landing lights ablaze. I quietly told Moon to take his time. Instead, I pivoted to the care workers who appeared out of place among all that desert camouflage. The first speaker came forward and stood at my side. He cut a strapping figure; I had wondered on occasion about spending a night with him.

"No one comes to Desperido by choice." I chuckled. "That's what they *used* to say, my friends. Now, it's a destination for Aztecans who no longer fit society's rigid mold. Some run here. Others hide. You lot have chosen to fight. For revenge, justice, pleasure. The reasons are endless. You share them here every night. *You* share them.

"But there's a problem. You're only a third of this town's population, and you wouldn't be here but for the hard work of the other two-thirds. Tonight, their voice enters the Circle. Treat them as you do your comrades: Do not judge. More to the point: Listen with open ears."

I handed Diego the ceremonial flask, and he sipped. I squeezed his arm and whispered.

"All yours, my friend."

He shocked me by agreeing to speak. Before the army arrived, our care workers knew more about the intimate behavior of their fellow contractors than anyone other than Lumen. They had serviced the majority at least once, and by all accounts maintained respectful relations. Alas, my soldiers saw prostitution in a different light.

He began simply, head held high.

"My name is Diego. A few of you know me. I have made my way for the past ten years servicing men and women. It is not the career I wanted for myself. I would bring shame to my family if they knew. My parents asked more of me than I could deliv … deliver."

Diego choked up but took a deep breath and recovered.

Good man.

"I fell into a life of crime. I was pathetic. When I was twenty-six and down to my final credits, I couldn't crawl back to my parents. A man told me of this place and offered to bring me here for a fee." Diego sighed. "Payable upfront. He stopped ten kilometers south of Machado and made me walk. Like I told you, I was pathetic.

"I arrived here with no money and no practical skills. The woman who used to run Desperido offered me a meal and a bed. Anything else, I'd have to earn. I soon met a care worker who said the town had no men in her profession. She said I would have many clients."

Diego closed his eyes and bowed his head. Was he remembering the first time? Was he terrified to go on?

"No job is beneath a man when he's run out of options. I'm not the only one here who's had to climb out of the gutter." Diego regained his composure and opened his eyes. "I'm not proud of my choices. I never will be. But I'm proud of what I give to others. A few moments of comfort, joy, a release from their burdens. I'm gentle, and I treat everyone who comes to my bed with respect.

"For ten years, my clients showed equal respect. Lately, that has changed. Not just for me. We have been physically and emotionally abused. We have been spit upon. We have been treated like punching bags. Some of us have been violated in the worst way."

I trained my eyes on the soldier who would soon have a role to play. He sneered with a wide, devilish grin. Many others squirmed. A few whispered to their neighbors. The uplifting atmosphere had long since vanished. They wondered why I gave Diego a forum.

"People like me came here to find refuge and to live in peace. There's nothing for me at the other end of Roadway 9. I'm not a warrior, but we are more alike than you know. All I ask is the respect I'm due."

Talk about awkward.

Diego had no big finish, nor did anyone applaud or cheer. He didn't experience that contrived nonsense where one person stood and clapped until others joined in. But he also received no jeers or laughs. And that, I concluded, was progress.

A buzzkill, for sure. But also progress.

He handed me the flask, which I rejected.

"For the next speaker, Diego."

He pivoted to the youngest care worker, who had waited her turn in the embrace of big Malva. Diego motioned her forward. They met halfway; she accepted the flask and sipped from it. She hesitated to move toward the Circle's center until I motioned to her landing spot.

"Here, Enid. In the best light. So everyone can see you."

Though her facial bruises had dissipated somewhat, they couldn't be missed. Compared to Diego, who dressed well and held his shoulders high, Enid came across like a wild child. Her dress was torn along the right side; her hair had not been brushed all day; and she didn't bother with makeup or jewelry. Her eyes were flush with tears.

She glanced at me, back again at her fellow care workers, and to the growing crowd which now included more than half the fighters and several dozen civilians. Per our agreement, Saul arranged for reps from every bunker to join the spectators. I caught Moon's tall silhouette toward the back of the crowd.

Enid did not follow my recommendation on how to begin.

"Some of you are animals."

The tone wasn't as harsh as the accusation. Enid had a tinny voice that made her seem twenty-five going on fifteen.

80

"I used to love my job. Lovemaking between two people is the most beautiful thing in the world, even when it's done for money. I had a gift. I ... I used to believe that. Like Diego said ... we were respected. We were part of this town. They were good neighbors. They treated us like friends.

"We welcomed you. I was so happy to have new clients. It was so beautiful, but you made it so ugly. So ..."

Enid froze. Her eyes fixated on our target. She'd been told to look for him in the crowd before speaking.

She pointed him out.

"You. You're an animal. You took everything from me."

The asshole in question glared this way and that, as if to pretend she was accusing a neighbor.

This fella was early forties, broad-shouldered with a crew cut and a scar running parallel beneath his jaw. Bett said he survived hand-to-hand with a Swarm F-grounder. Brilliant with a knife, she said. Spent half his post-war life in and out of mental facilities. Her intel suggested he pulled himself together.

Not entirely, it seemed.

Enid spat through her fury.

"I never used to carry a weapon. Next time, I'll gut you."

Probably not the best way to challenge someone trained in the art of slicing and dicing.

The man rose to his feet, fists to his side. Time to intervene. I grabbed the flask and whispered:

"That will suffice, Enid. Leave the rest to me."

She trembled through her rage but retreated as ordered.

OK, time for a hard lesson. I hated having to remind humans how to be civil, but they were so damn bad at it. Once again, a god to the rescue.

"Earlier, friends, I said we were not whole. The grievances you just heard are legitimate and partly representative of the larger chasm between the veterans of Desperido and the veterans of the

Swarm war. Tonight, we bridge the chasm, but not with convivial dialogue, shaking of hands, or songs of reconciliation."

I motioned the offending soldier forward.

"Max Grillo, stand beside me."

He held his ground. Oh, so that's how he wanted to play it.

"What for, Raul? What have I done?"

"Max, should I describe your crimes in front of everyone?"

He held his chin up. I think he was prepared to fight. Good.

"Ain't done no crime. You saying I hurt them whores?"

Eh. This fella lacked any semblance of linquistic discipline.

"Come to my side, Max, and let's find a solution."

"No. I'm leaving. Ain't got to hear this shit."

I'm sure he was deathly afraid, but a clever man faces the hard truth without exposing his frailty. Not Max.

I saw inside his mind and grabbed hold of the neural commands which governed mobility. Ixoca once demonstrated how to manipulate my way through the human brain's complex synaptic network. "Take care," he warned. "A misguided attempt to control muscle movement can produce a deadly aneurysm."

Max turned to leave, but his body refused. His legs bent awkwardly toward me, like a puppet whose master had just begun learning how to pull the strings. Max resisted; his eyes ballooned in terror. He knew I was in control. Everyone did.

"I made a simple request, my friend. Please don't fight me. Come. Stand by my side."

The fighters nearby encouraged him to follow my orders, which came from the top of his chain of command. Max conceded. As soon as he moved toward me under his own power, I released my hold.

"Now we might begin to heal. First, all of you should know that Max is not the only one guilty of violations against our care workers. Nor is he the only soldier to show disrespect to our civilian population.

"In fact, a significant divide exists between those who live above ground and those who do not. This is unacceptable. We are nine hundred souls who have chosen to separate ourselves from the trials and degradations of a society bound by regulation, limitation, and discrimination. By walking this path, society paints us to be outcasts, exiles, criminals, derelicts, misfits.

"All nine hundred. Together. One community apart from the rest. For now, *we* are the outlaws. In time, and with your relentless fervor, *they* will be the outlaws. To achieve this end, we must embrace each other as equal partners. Sure, we have a command structure — I seek chaos, not anarchy. But we do not divide ourselves by class. A man who wields a blast rifle will not take advantage of a man who only wishes to provide comfort."

I didn't rehearse the speech, but it gave me the tingles. Even better, it made quite the impression. I saw it in their faces, lit by the lamp's glow. Jaws agape, eyes fixed on their glorious leader, heads nodding in approval. Almost as many civilians surrounded the Circle as military. They'd report to the others what they saw.

Time to demonstrate the consequences for shattering our unity.

"Max, you stand accused of multiple heinous crimes against your fellow Desperidans. I won't describe your violations because you know them. Plus, we have no system of justice that requires I state the charges. And, as you've already pleaded not guilty to any crime, I'm left only to pass sentence based on witness testimony."

It's amazing how a man can change his tune when he sees no way out. Max flicked his eyes toward the care workers. He seemed less sinister.

"Raul. Boss. Look ... I'm sorry. I lost my head. I promise ... won't do none of that again."

"Yes. I'd agree. You won't do it again. But an apology does not excuse the behavior. I'm afraid, Max, you've been chosen to bear the pain for all transgressions against these Desperidans." I raised my voice to ensure everyone heard. "Let this be the last time we stand divided. We will wage war against our enemies, but we will not harm each other. We are nine hundred. We are one."

Max was the one they focused upon.

I started where justice demanded. I altered the blood temperature inside his scrotum and sent a burning spear into his penis.

Max bent over, grabbed his private zone, and fell to his knees. He whimpered like a child.

"Agh. Puh … please. Make it stop."

"Did your victims say something similar?"

"I'm sorry. I …"

My eyes shifted to Bett, who I placed in arguably the second most uncomfortable spot. She couldn't defend Max because she agreed to this punishment. I wanted to kill him, as the strictest possible warning. She pushed back, saying a death sentence for a crime less than murder or treason would break the spell we held over these soldiers. Saul concurred. Ah, sour compromise.

Next, he felt a disturbance in his anus. It became agonizing, as if shards of glass poured through his colon. Max howled as he collapsed into a heap. I glanced over my shoulder toward Enid. Her disdain for this malgado struggled to hold up against her disgust at what she saw.

Revenge never tastes as sweet as we expect.

Enid, Diego, and the other care workers chose Max. I asked them to determine the one man whose crimes were most egregious, that he alone would bear the price.

While I was at times excessive in punishing my enemies, no one could accuse me of being capricious. On the contrary, I inflicted pain and death with purpose and discipline. That night in the Circle, I walked a careful line between proper proportion and excess. I didn't let go of Max until I emptied his bladder.

What remained was a wet stain in his pants and public humiliation, but the physical pain vanished. He'd never be the same. He'd never fight for me or be trusted in this community. I'd wipe his memory later.

He cried at my feet while I addressed my people.

"Max Grillo stands as the face of what happens when we do not act as one. May he be the first and last member of the new Desperido to face punishment for a crime against one of our own. When you leave here tonight, talk to each other about the power of unity. Tomorrow night, welcome anyone into this Circle. When you see each other in the cantina, invite strangers to share a drink.

"Likewise, I say to my six hundred contractors: This town is no longer yours alone. Reach out to these beautiful men and women who will protect you from the enemy. Hear their stories. Know their journeys. See that the pain which brought them here is no different than yours. From now, we are one. We are Black Star. We do not hurt our own. Disperse, my friends, and have a lovely night."

On the positive: No one argued, sneered, or cursed. And no one came to Max's aid. On the negative: Only a handful applauded.

Eh. Can't have it all.

They dispersed slowly, a few nods between the fighters and the civilians. It wasn't funereal, but the evening was young. I suspected the cantina staff would remain busy deep into the night.

I did catch Diego mouth the words *thank you* as he left. Big Malva, the senior care worker, followed suit.

This was new territory for me. In retrospect, it was a lovely exhibition but not something I hoped to repeat. A quick, matter-of-fact execution made the point without fanfare.

Max sat up on one knee by the time Bett, Moon, and Saul huddled with me several feet away. I asked for their thoughts.

Bett glanced at Max.

"I'll know more by morning."

Saul took a more philosophical perspective.

"Either you opened their eyes and their hearts, or you set the literal fear of god in them. Terror for what you and Ilan can do to them will not produce the unity you seek."

"Agreed, my friend. This was a gamble, but I don't believe in half measures. Still, you might advise the care workers to keep a knife nearby, in case of reprisals. Ilan?"

Moon puffed the last of his cigar.

"We'll be fine. As soon as they see vids from Bolivar, our fighters will be reminded what Black Star is accomplishing. Rotate the newbies into the field for our next mission. Give everyone a taste of combat. It's infectious. They'll fall in line."

Bett reached for another cheroot.

"Ilan's right. They need a fucking taste."

"No worries, Stopper. After everything we set in motion today, I guarantee we'll soon be fighting many enemies. We ..."

Max stumbled toward us, fists raised in defiant fury.

"Raul, you cunt! You got no right to ..."

His eyes rolled back in his head, and Max twirled a half-turn before he collapsed. Bett started toward him.

"What? Did you kill ...?"

"No, no. He briefly lost oxygen to his brain. The next time he wakes, Max will find himself at a transport station in Machado. The last few months will have never happened."

I could have killed him en route. Bett never would've known. Yet somehow, that seemed like a betrayal of my good word.

Imagine. Me keeping promises to someone other than Moon. I told Ship the truth about his journey, as confessed by Lumen. I told Bett that Max would only suffer a brief humiliation before I set him free.

Had I become too accommodating? Too trustworthy?

Later that night, after I left Max with a hole in his mind and a few credits to his name, Moon and I retreated to the bunker we shared for six months. We discussed the state of our campaign. We rambled and schemed until sunrise, when I said:

"Moon, you once accused me of becoming soft. I think you might've been right. I'm earnest more often than not. I'm almost ..."

I didn't dare utter the word. Nor did Moon.

Yeah, no. Wasn't going to allow that shit to happen. Fortunately, the tide of history would soon permit me to escape my inexorable slide toward humanity.

10

THE PRESIDENT OF THE COLLECTORATE and I went way back. One might say we were briefly allies of convenience – then and now. Friends, we were not. Didn't see life the same way. As a human, I killed a few of her family members and almost blew up her ship days later. Not a great way to build bridges. However, I did save her life and the universe as she knew it late in my godhood, so she owed me the farm. Naturally, I collected.

Shortly after Ixoca bestowed me with the gift of many eyes, I filtered out the insignificant peons, leaving them for the Jewel, and kept a close watch on President Kara Aleksanyan. She'd provide me with extraordinary amounts of intelligence vital to my goals. Or so I presumed. She'd show me how the Collectorate functioned at its highest levels. Or so I predicted. Naively.

Alas, my insight was limited to whatever Chief of Staff Kai Parke saw and heard. Mostly, that amounted to the mundane business of the executive office and much political hand-wringing with allies and opponents from the Interstellar Congress.

Wannabe gods fighting for every scrap of power.

The Prez did not include the Chief of Staff in meetings with top commanders from the UNF and SI. Every time Prez closed the door on Kai Parke, I sensed the man's resentment. We were entitled to better access. We earned that shit.

Yet I never pushed Kai into the background. Our fate was tied to the President, who only had a few months to live – assuming the timeline did not shift. I discerned only Kai and Security Chief Leonard Baldwin knew about us. Leonard arrived at the Fort of Inarra three years ago with then Vice-President Aleksanyan to set our arrangement into motion. I didn't know about Kai's involvement until Ixoca first previewed his many eyes.

Those three developed a verbal shorthand. A careful study of their coded language warned me of critical meetings. Moon and I listened carefully in the days after we took out our targets at Conquillos Base and delivered proof to the drop at 40-Cignus. Finally, ten days after the mission and as we prepared to ramp up new off-world Motif operations, we heard the long-expected dialogue.

Leonard arrived in the President's outer office, where Kai calmed a group of activists who demanded an audience with the great lady. Something about the latest environmental law endangering their tribal homes on ...

Blah, blah, and blah.

Leonard motioned Kai away and spoke under his breath.

"The President is tired. She's in need of quiet time with a cup of tea and a Kohlna roll."

Kai responded, "Right away."

That was the signal. Kai told the uninvited guests that the President had retired to her personal quarters for the day. They didn't believe his bullshit, of course, but a security team escorted them off the premises.

Leonard and Kai entered the President's office and made themselves at home. She tossed away the wall of holos hovering above her desk.

"It never ends," Kara said. "Tell me you have good news, Leonard."

"A mixed bag, Madame President."

"Don't say it. More collateral losses?"

Leonard crossed his legs.

"A few, yes. But don't concern yourself about public outrage. This is nothing like Qasi Ransome."

"Explain."

"Our friends provided visual proof: The targets are dead. Anton Cherry and Reynaldo Barron will no longer pose a threat."

If Kara was relieved, she demonstrated no sign. She could've at least been thankful for our outstanding work.

"That's supposed to be good news. Why should I be worried?"

Leonard opened his pom and retrieved data we left at the drop.

"Madame President, I collected this information five days ago. It didn't sit right with me, so I reached out to my contacts on Azteca."

"What's wrong?"

"First, there's the matter of Judge Barron. Officially, he's not dead. The man left for a private retreat. According to our friends, his body will be found in a few days. It will look like suicide."

Kai intervened.

"I don't see the problem so far, Leonard. He's out of our hair."

"True. But the same day he disappeared, the Judge issued a reversal on his longstanding opposition to a greater planetary role for SI and the UNF. For years, he ruled in favor of Aztecan internal sovereignty. This about-face makes no sense."

Kara nodded. "Unless his ruling was coerced."

"Almost certainly."

"Were our friends involved?"

"They made no mention of it here. Later I learned that the provincial governor, Martin Jimenez, resigned the same day Anton Cherry died and Judge Barron issued his ruling."

Kara grabbed her digipipe and double-tapped it to light.

"Jimenez? I met him last year at the IC Trade Forum. I only remember because he was a cold bastard. He wouldn't let go of my hand without crucifying my intersystem commerce policies. Was he closely aligned with the targets?"

"Oh, yes. They were a fearsome trio. Jimenez was serving his fifth term. I've been watching the political fallout. His resignation caught everyone off-guard. His likely successor carries a strong pro-Collectorate voice."

Kara pulled on the digipipe.

"Did Jimenez explain his resignation?"

"No. And he's disappeared from the public eye. There's another strange twist. Maris Sylva, the head of UniShip Global, was found dead on Conquillos Base, not far from Mr. Cherry."

"Sylva? Never met her. What were she and Cherry doing there?"

"That required considerable research. It appears she wanted to revoke the UNF's fifty-year lease on the property. To what end, we can't say. But Mr. Cherry's presence would suggest he wanted it for a staging ground. At first, I thought Sylva was a collateral loss. Wrong place, wrong time. Our friends didn't mention her in their report."

Kara leaned back and pulled on her digipipe.

"What did you find?"

"She had worked out a deal with UNF Ground Operations to surrender the lease. It did not go through official channels."

"Payoffs?"

"No doubt. Here's the wrinkle, Madame President. The day she died, Sylva sent a deepstream to Ground Ops expressing a total reversal. She told them to hold onto the lease and send reps to Azteca."

"For what purpose?"

"She claimed anti-Collectorate factions might use Conquillos for violent means."

The Prez threw up her hands. And why not?

"None of this makes sense, Leonard. Cherry, Barron, Jimenez, Sylva. The same day." She turned to Kai. "What do you make of this?"

"From a political standpoint, it's a perfect intersection," the Chief of Staff said. "Four important voices either silenced or converted. This sort of thing would normally act like a fresh infusion of Carbedyne. We'd run with it."

"But?"

Kai grunted. "It stinks, Madame President. I smell it from seventy light-years away. I'm sure the locals are raising ten kinds of hell."

Indeed, politicos, stream pundits, and intersectional constables were busy investigating not only the murders but also the mass disappearances of several folks employed by the dead.

"You think our friends are behind it?" Kara asked Kai.

"Probably, but I can't see why. They were commissioned to take out Cherry and Barron. Nothing more."

"Leonard?"

The Security Chief closed his pom.

"I agree with Kai. They went far beyond the parameters, which means our friends are playing a different game."

Bravo, my friend. Did you ever believe otherwise?

"What's their objective? If I hear you correctly, Leonard, it sounds like they're improving conditions on the ground for our side. But those two have no interest in politics."

The Prez hit that point square on the noggin.

"Which is what worries me, Kara. They far exceeded parameters on Qasi Ransome, but there were no repercussions beyond the deaths themselves. Now, they appear to be orchestrating external events. After Qasi, I recommended we cut the cord. You refused. The longer we engage them, we put ourselves at risk."

"Kai? Do you agree?"

My host sighed long and hard.

"I've always been straight with you, Madame President. I won't change now. Our friends have removed genuine threats. We still haven't found Q6, but we're cutting the legs out of his network. I recommend we stay the course."

Leonard objected until Kai cut him off.

"But we change up our strategy."

"How so, Kai?"

"One of us needs to make face to face contact. Demand an explanation. If we knew their motivation ..."

"No." Leonard snapped. "The drop is too high a risk as is. If anyone ever connected this office to Royal and Moon ..."

Yes! The first time I heard those assholes mention us by name.

"They won't." Kara shot back. "We'll maintain the same routine, Leonard. Look, Kai's right. We have to know what they're planning. If our goals and theirs don't align, then we go our separate ways. If they don't pose a threat to this administration, we work with them until we expose Q6."

Oh, dear. That was going to be difficult. Q6 *was* behind a conspiracy, but not the one she believed.

"I disagree, Kara, but I'm here to serve. Your orders?"

The Prez mulled it over for a moment, consuming that sweet leaf.

"Send the beacon, Leonard. The next time they visit the drop, I want you there. Ask for a meeting on the asteroid inside their ship."

He shook his head.

"They'll think it's a trap."

"Convince them it's not. You'll go alone. Unarmed. Tell them to keep their worm drive catalyzed and take you hostage if anyone else enters the system."

"What about the timing? In the past, they responded to the beacon within hours or waited for days. If I arrive while they're in 40-Cignus, they'll know we're watching the drop."

Ouch.

I often wondered if they hid some surveillance tools in the nearby region. Bart ran searches every time but turned up nothing.

"Leonard, we're forty-eight minutes away by worm. That won't give us enough lead time. But we have alternatives. Ask SI for help."

"Dangerous, but I can make it work."

93

"Good." Kara massaged her forehead. "Anything else to report?"

"You know the gist, Madame President."

She tapped off the digipipe.

"Fine. You two sort it. And please, don't antagonize our friends. We still need them. There are so many brushfires and so little time."

"Not a problem," Kai said. "We'll handle it."

How nice. I'd have to keep a tethered eye toward their clandestine meeting. I couldn't wait to hear the details.

When the Prez dismissed her co-conspirators, I relied on my oldest and dearest of friends to assess. Moon watched the meeting from our bunker in Desperido, while I enjoyed it on Bolivar aboard our revamped new Scramjet Maria. Soon, I'd return home to complete her maiden voyage.

"They're flying blind," Moon said. "They still believe Q6 is one of them. And they got no idea we're a hundred steps ahead."

"True. But her Chief of Staff is correct. People in that region are, as he said, raising hell. When they find the Judge, fingers will be pointed and long knives will be sharpened."

"With all signs pointing to SI and the UNF, partner. It's what Ixoca wanted."

Couldn't argue with Moon's assertion.

"True, but it's the opposite of what our fighters thought they accomplished."

As usual, Moon inundated his words in a large cloud of smoke.

"We knew playing both sides would be a risk, but who can argue with the result?"

Indeed. By week's end, we'd commit two-thirds of our army to four off-world missions, with plans for another three inside the next sixty days. Before long, Desperido would become an outpost rather than our central command.

"No argument here, my friend. But I think it best we keep our people busy and on the move. The less time they have to consider our true agenda, all the better. What do you think about a meetup with Leonard?"

Moon grumbled.

"Hard to say, Royal. You're the only one he's ever met."

"If you could call it that. I might have said ten words."

"That wasn't your fault, partner. Leonard never did care for this arrangement. I told you we should've killed him when we had the chance. The President would've found someone more flexible."

Moon and I rarely disagreed in recent months.

"I doubt it, my friend. That man is loyal to the death. If she wasn't married with children, he'd likely propose. I see it in his eyes. The one that got away."

"Leonard has extensive contacts in SI. He might decide it's better to take us out before we cause more trouble."

The thought had crossed my mind.

"Possible. But we have the tactical advantage. We're prepared for any curve. To increase our chances, I'll go by myself."

"You actually believe he'll say anything worth hearing?"

A familiar gaggle of laughter erupted outside the Scramjet. My passengers approached.

"I do. Let's talk more after the party."

Moon laughed. Oh, how I loved to hear that sound.

"It's going to be a blowout, partner. They're decorating the avenue."

My passengers hopped onboard, led by the Collectorate's most flamboyant young drug lord. I took one look at Elian and told Moon:

"Make sure our folks don't overdo the adulation. He's already quite full of himself."

Speaking as a long-time narcissist, I knew when someone had exceeded the reasonable, preset limits of his ego.

"See you soon, my friend."

I asked my fighters to take their still-seats then powered on the navigation circle. We'd enter worm in less than sixty seconds. At the far end of our journey? A welcome home celebration likely to last through the night.

Good times, indeed.

Yet I never took my eyes off Kai Parke. The real fun was happening far away at the center of the galactic government. What did he and Leonard have in store for me?

11

ELIAN ENTERED MY LIFE the day we landed Bart in town for the first time. He approached us agog at the sight of my gorgeous interstellar sedan and peppered me with questions only a techno-nerd thought intriguing. He didn't see the potential for his quaint little drug until I opened his eyes. When I added him to the table, no one offered a more enthusiastic "Yes, boss" and "Gotcha, boss."

Oh, how six months can transform a man.

He returned home aboard Maria with ten of his team – six soldiers from the first Bolivar rotation plus four Motif designers – and spent most of the journey regaling them with tales of the future while I listened from the Nav circle.

"Half a billion steady clients in one year," he promised. "We set production levels at fifty percent capacity and triple the price. They'll be fighting each other for the product. We're looking at a valuation of two billion UCVs."

His audience salivated at the numbers. But wait, there was more!

"Best part, my people? That's a six-planet projection with no more than two facilities on each."

"It's exciting," said Leia, who was Elian's top designer and, by my estimation, one of four current lovers. "I'm not the best with numbers, but couldn't we explode our valuation if we operated at a higher capacity?"

Elian took the critique in stride. He massaged his goatee, which he manicured at least twice a day. He sculpted a new appearance several times a month. Spiked yellow hair one week, neon green locks the next. Along the way, he became obsessed with earrings. Today, he settled for emerald studs.

"Now see, Leia, that's where short-term math can deceive. If we flood the night market with twice the product in the same window? Sure, we'll suck in a bigger haul. But too many clients too fast dilutes the mystery. Right now, we got a product that sounds too good to be true. Word is spreading to planets we ain't even touched."

The young king flailed his arms with a kinetic energy that I must admit was downright infectious. I used to be the same way at his age. At some point, I learned a good salesman needed only to master language delivered in a comforting tone with an unassuming smile. Elian would get there someday. He rambled on.

"Our best long-term sales tool? Whispers. Rumors. Gossip. People need to be flapping their lips. After a spell, those quiet voices will turn to a clamor. They'll hear reports about constabulary raids on Motif hot houses, and the UNF seizing smugglers. Yeah, my people. We'll take some hits, but that's gonna be damn fine for business. Free publicity. In the meantime, we keep expanding but not so fast we flood the market. If we do, the mystery ends and prices fall. Right, Raul?"

Oh, good. He thought to include me.

"Right, Raul?"

It lacked the reverence of, say, "Tell her I'm correct, boss."

Elian still deferred to my authority in private settings, but he knew the public score. He rapidly approached legendary status, ranking more or less alongside us actual gods. Sure, we lifted him up, expanded his business opportunities, removed his one impediment to space travel, and allowed him free reign to kill anybody who stood in the way of Motif production. One might suggest we created a monster, but one would be wrong. Elian was simply another human too big for his goddamn britches.

To be fair, they were highly profitable britches, giving life to our ambition on an accelerated timetable. Our six hundred contractors and three hundred soldiers benefited with every new client and production facility. His genius, fueled by the occasional psychotic episode, turned him into a larger-than-life figure among our constituency. While Moon and I might have transformed Desperido, Elian became the true pied piper. He allowed his status to bludgeon whatever humility he once possessed.

He wore the same camouflage as the soldiers, insisting he train and fight alongside them whenever his busy schedule did not interfere. If the vets were given a choice to follow Elian or Bett, the vote might be close.

I didn't dislike the new Elian. He was happy. He loved life. But I knew where this path led, and I damn well wasn't about to correct his course.

When he asked me to verify his thoughts about the economics of flooding the night market too soon, I shrugged.

"Humans love to be seduced, my friends. Long, protracted foreplay only whets the appetite. Yes, Elian. You're correct."

All he wanted was a simple "yes." He barely acknowledged my affirmation and jumped into another extended ramble, where he extrapolated a long-term vision for his empire.

"In three years, we'll be worth a hundred billion creds. At that point, we'll license the formula. Every MedCorps and Pharma Research Division will pay for the binding agent so they can treat the addiction."

"Unless they crack our code sooner," Leia said.

Elian chuckled. "C'mon, now. You know that ain't happening."

"Not if we maintain quality control."

Manny Tua, one of the first fighters to join our original three vets, agreed with Leia.

"Got to be careful, boss. Only need one reckless designer to leave the backdoor open."

Elian nodded. He knew the risk. If competitors designed a superior product for a better price, the empire might fall as quickly as it rose.

"I'm working that angle every day, Manny. Got my team back in Desperido designing the next iteration. Soon as somebody dumps inferior shit on the market, we'll wipe the floor with those malgados. You beat the market by staying ahead of it. And my people? I taught them everything I know. Ain't nothing but glitter."

Ah, yes. Elian. Bountiful confidence that would one day become a symbol for "famous last words."

Until then, I hoped he continued to have fun. A short life as radiant as the sun surpassed a long one mired in a perpetual fog.

We arrived home shortly before sunset. Elian disembarked Maria to a hero's cheer. A healthy blend of civilians and soldiers made way for Elian and his team.

The intermingled crowd pleased me. All that drama in the Circle ten days earlier had served a vital purpose. Though we did lose five good soldiers who couldn't abide by the new terms, the rest appeared to embrace an integrated Desperido. Saul reported only a few arguments and one fight inside the cantina. The care workers resumed an active schedule of pleasing encounters.

Ironically, the drug that put us on the map would someday threaten to implode humanity's oldest profession. Anyone looking for the ultimate sexual pleasure need only grab the nearest Motif wafer. "An indescribable experience" claimed the humans who tried it and came back for more. And more.

We banned the sale and use of the drug inside our lovely little town. The last thing we needed were addicts of any kind. And although the drug only killed clients at a four percent clip, our population could not afford to take a hit of that size. We wanted contractors working at peak efficiency and fighters to face the enemy with a clear mind.

Which meant our town honored Elian solely for how much money he made for them. Sudden wealth had a convenient way of pushing morality aside. If the Motif market collapsed, his supplicants would vanish on the wind.

Eh. Typical.

Central avenue came alive with hanging glow lamps, Aztecan traditional dance music, and the smell of smoked beef. My olfactory sensors confirmed: Someone purchased a side of Hanta-cow. Gram for gram, the most expensive meat for eighty light-years.

"Good to know people are spending their credits wisely," I told Moon as we joined the celebration. "Who's the fool?"

Moon chuckled. "Elian. He ordered it from Bolivar six days ago. Right down to specifications for how it was to be butchered."

"Interesting. I remember when our young hero only ate from his hydrogarden."

Moon tucked his cigar between his teeth.

"We had a conversation on that subject recently. He converted while setting up the Minivet facility on Inuit Kingdom. The locals live mostly on a diet of bread and herbed bear meat. He ate what they served him and dreamed about it every night. Or so he describes it. Now, he's a full-fledged carnivore."

I couldn't have cared less, but the advantage seemed clear.

"All the top predators eat flesh, my friend."

"Elian is fast becoming one of the best."

Moon said those words with genuine admiration. At some point shortly after Ixoca entered our lives and Desperido began expanding Motif operations, Moon discovered a sharp, relatable edge in Elian. He liked the young maestro's blasé approach to how many millions of people Motif would someday kill. But of even greater fascination, he took a fancy to Elian's grace under pressure.

He spoke with considerable regard after a mission where we briefly ran afoul of smugglers who demanded unreasonable fees for hauling our products off world. At the time, our private worm travel was limited to Bart, and we were outgrowing the road trains.

The three of us faced the President, Vice-President, and Financial Auditor for an outfit called Emway Rightway. Now, these folks were about as respectable as the cargo they hauled, and their company name existed in no official registries.

Boss Emway was a toady little creature with an oversized mouth. His partner, Boss Rightway, was a string-bean creation who provided a perfect visual contrast. The Auditor, known only as Madame Swain, obsessed with a tablet and rarely looked up.

We hadn't negotiated for ten minutes when we realized these malgados weren't going to ship our products until they received a permanent cut of the action. Being a sensible non-human, I considered several potential compromises. A concession need not equal defeat. Elian disagreed and made his position clear.

"It's like this, Emway. You reckon we won't find a better deal with your competitors."

"I know you won't," the pear-shaped rat replied. "But if you bring me in, you're guaranteed smooth sailing for a decade. The others can't match that claim."

Elian, sitting between Moon and I at a table with a lovely lakeview, gigged us with his elbows.

"How about this malgado? He just doesn't get it. We ain't out here selling shares. What about you, Rightway? Toeing the company line?"

Stringbean sipped a delightful café (admittedly, their staff did use the best beans). He sighed long and deep, as if bored with the affair.

"Our offer is reasonable. If you wish to command the interstellar market, you *will* go through us."

The arrogant shit should have known better. Then again, what happened next surprised everyone present.

Elian snickered. "You guys are out of your league. Allow me to set the terms."

He leapt from his chair, grabbed his pistol, which he turned sideways in his trigger hand. A gauche technique, but it did the trick. Elian delivered one laser bolt through each man's heart. Rightway dropped his café, and Emway slumped forward. Then he farted.

Madame Swain suddenly paid attention, though the trauma was too much for words. She must have been shocked when Elian holstered his pistol.

Elian told us, "Now we're dealing with the credit goddess. She'll set us up with a sugary deal. Whatcha say, Madame Swain? You're the new President of Emway Rightway."

Our young virtuoso wielded a blunt hammer. Not the best tool at a negotiating table, but we never ordered him *not* to kill anyone. He thought on his feet. Moon admired the decisive action. No long-winded smooth talking, no suave and debonair manipulation. That wasn't Moon's game. Never had been.

Moon and Elian found common ground. Soon thereafter, they frequented adjacent stools at the cantina bar, and Elian took to smoking the same class of cigars. These days he walked around in a familiar cloud of smoke.

I should've felt jealous. Moon found a friend not named Royal.

Never thought I'd live to see the day.

How about that?

After much backslapping, handshaking, and general cajoling upon our return, Elian spoke to the gathered citizenry of Desperido.

"It's great to be home, my people!"

He once tried to adopt 'my friends' as his preferred linquistic shoutout, but I claimed territorial rights. He didn't think long on the alternative. Eh.

"I used to hate this town," he continued. "But every time I'm out there among the stars, I can't get back here fast enough."

Now that was an outright lie. Only last night, Elian suggested we speed up the expansion timetable because he never wanted to see red dust on his shoes again. He propped up his feet on a table as he pulled on a massive black cigar and spoke of the coming months.

"Raul, we need to scout for a permanent base of operations. I want something in paradise. There's gotta be lots of water. And birds. The tall, skinny ones with the big wings. Forget their name."

I nursed my favorite whiskey and played along.

"Ah. I see. Let's go for egrets. Now, what about the estate? Should we start from scratch or make an offer?"

He considered my questions through short, rapid puffs.

"Don't want to build. Takes too long, Raul."

"Ah. So we buy, my friend. Any architectural preferences? Castles? Forts? How much acreage? Keep in mind: A huge estate will require significant security measures and a hefty pay stamp for all the support personnel. Throw out a number."

"Based on the Common Currency Standard, I'd say we shoot for six million creds."

Real estate was *not* Elian's game.

"So that would be a down payment. Yes? Then we'd have to sort out a budget for security, staff, maintenance, plus a payoff structure for the regional constabulary." When his smile faded, I piled on. "If *permanent* and *paradise* are the baseline, my friend, I'd shoot for thirty million upfront and an annual pay stamp of at least forty million."

He crimped his lips.

"Sounds pricey."

"Oh, I'm sure we'd get a better deal on Bolivar, say, than Earth or Catalan. But Bolivar is not known for its paradisical qualities."

"True. And I don't want to live in the mountains with those people. Talk about the refuse of humanity."

He had no idea how far his species could fall, but I appreciated the snobbery. I taught him a thing or two.

"On the bright side, my friend, you'll be worth ten times that in two years. At some point, you might even turn your eye to purchasing entire towns. It's been known to happen."

He sat up straight.

"Really? That's a thing?"

"I took Desperido and never signed a deed."

"Oh. Yes. Forgot about that. But I'm not a god. Although ..." His fingers outlined that perfectly coiffed goatee. "We could have anything we want. Show up with enough soldiers – hey, what are they gonna do? The UNF won't get involved."

I asked him if the poor residents would be enslaved, forcibly migrated, or exterminated. His answer did not match my prediction.

"Obviously, we couldn't kill them all. Essential workers. The ones that keep the lights on and the water running. Folks like that."

"Ah. And when they've taught us how to be self-sufficient ..."

Elian shrugged. "Can't have witnesses. They'd run off to find help. Nah. After we clean house, nothing but glitter."

Spoken like a genuine psychopath.

Those people tended to have short life spans.

After Elian finished lying to the crowd about his fondness for Desperido, he asked everyone to raise a glass and offered a toast.

"To my nine hundred comrades. Thank you for honoring our latest victory. But this is just the groundwork. We're going to conquer every corner of the Collectorate. Hail, Black Star!"

Short, sweet, inspirational. A little hyperbolic, perhaps.

It did the trick, ensuring this party would have long life.

Actually, I enjoyed seeing Elian and his team garner attention. Standing at the center of universal adulation is a tiring exercise. Instead, I backed away with my drink and found an observational huddle with Saul, Bett, and Moon.

"Quite a change from the day we arrived," I told anyone listening.

"I remember it well," Saul said. "You and Ilan accompanied by Evelyn Cardinale's men. I must confess: I didn't think you two would leave Desperido alive."

Moon laughed. "I just wanted to leave, but my partner had a grand revelation about this town. I thought he lost his mind."

I swigged the sweet golden beverage.

"Always trust in the wisdom of Raul Torreta."

Bett responded just as she did the day we met onboard Road Train 1492.

"If that's your name."

I wouldn't say Bett and I had sealed the wounds from that day's misadventure. I never formally apologized; thus she never forgave me. But she left behind her old life and any allegiances. She loved commanding an army, a dream the UNF never offered. As for Black Star's filthy laundry?

Stopper accepted the cold, hard reality: We'd always be steeped in blood. We'd leave bodies on the deck.

"As long as every mission has identifiable objectives and doesn't involve suicide," she told me when I offered her tactical command, "I'm in. Whatever needs to be done. Fuck the rest of it."

Damn, I loved her spirit.

"Tell you what, my friends. Why don't the four of us find a nice, quiet place and have a private celebration?"

Moon's frown suggested he didn't want to leave the party, a truly remarkable personality switch.

"I've never seen Desperido this alive, Raul. And you want to leave?"

"I don't think we'll be missed. Not one of us."

Bett and Saul concurred.

"We are not under the glow tonight," Saul said.

Stopper reached for a cheroot.

"Whatcha have in mind?"

"How about we huddle in Bart? Enjoy a few drinks. Discuss the future. Moon and I saw something of great interest in the President's office today. There's a storm coming, my friends. It's always good to review storm preparation. Yes?"

Saul nodded. "Preparation is the art of repetition."

"Not to mention, our next campaigns are a week out," Stopper said. "We'll be stretching manpower thinner than ever."

Moon sighed. "Agreed. This might be the last party for a long time."

As a flurry of events soon proved, my partner's assessment was spot-on.

12

S IX DAYS LATER, THE FULL TABLE of trust met for a final planning session before we expanded our operations to two more planets.

We gathered inside Desperido Control, a module built close to the northern perimeter. In one room, a small team monitored our defense systems and sighter-drone relays up to twenty kilometers in every direction. They opened and closed the shield as necessary and tracked all comms in and out of town. The table of trust assembled in the adjacent room.

Elian wanted to jump right into the logistics of our upcoming setup on Indonesia Prime and G'hladi. The young king craved new glory now that the afterglow of the Bolivar victory had faded. He opened his pom and prepared to review plans.

From my exalted position at one end of the table, I wagged a dismissive finger and politely asked him to sit. Had he forgotten protocol? The real gods had the first word. Always.

"Patience, my friend. Breaking news of some consequence took place while you slept. These headlines will impact our timeline, although precisely how is not yet clear. Don't forget: Though we look skyward, our work here is far from finished. Ilan and I made a commitment to Ixoca and our Aztecan veterans. We would not have come so far so fast without them."

Stopper, Tracer, and Inky nodded their appreciation. They wanted to eliminate the homegrown threat to Azteca before committing their lives solely to a Collectorate-wide enterprise.

I gave the floor to Moon, who felt more comfortable these days in a public speaking role. He displayed images gathered from the Aztecan global stream and a special source inside the Children of Orpheus.

"Last night, twenty-two people died at a storage facility a couple hundred kilometers northeast of Machado. Officially, the regional constabulary says it's a cartel turf war. But the Deputy Constable who's overseeing the investigation is one of Ixoca's generals. Our common friend made a request for all the records. Raul and I received these vids an hour ago."

The carnage suggested more than a mere shootout. Fires burned throughout the facility, which had been bombarded from the air. Many of the dead lay scattered in several pieces.

"What happened there?" Tracer asked. "Looks like the Swarm war all over again."

Elian chuckled. "Or when we took out the Pezos clan."

"That's the point," Moon said. "This was a military-style assault. The constabulary says the weapons were likely UNF-issue. Some might date back to the peacekeeper years."

Bett rapped the table.

"Must be the arsenal Anton Cherry stockpiled for a few decades. Perhaps the weapons he entrusted to a certain Poros Cartel."

"Correct," I said. "At Conquillos, I instructed Senor Limon, the solicitor for Esteban Poros, to convince his boss of the value in off-loading those weapons to the Horax."

"Yep, and Limon said Poros would demand compensation."

"It appears negotiations to that effect had begun but ended poorly." I pointed to the bloody images. "Very. Poorly. Limon's body was identified. So was Mateo Cardinale's cousin Santiago, his right hand."

"Who ambushed whom?" Genoa asked.

Moon regained control of the presentation.

"The Horax took the brunt, but they were also the instigators. Our best theory is they lowballed Poros. The offer was rejected. The Horax set up another meeting between Cardinale and Limon, but they had no intention of paying even one credit."

Elian jumped in. "So, they arrived locked and loaded, figuring to take out the Poros crew and claim the arsenal free of charge. Their plan backfired. They took it up the ass."

Moon nodded. "When Cardinale's people opened fire, the enemy surprised them with bigger guns and air support."

Ship's first words to me went straight to the heart of the matter:

"This is good news for us. Right, boss?"

"Potentially even better, my friend. Our goal was to stir all-out war between the cartels. If they're fighting each other, they can't put their weight behind the factions who want to ignite a global insurrection. And they ignore the threat from Desperido. I never expected Poros to dump his arsenal for any price, but this result occurred much faster than I forecasted."

"Will that pose a problem for my expansion?" Elian asked.

I made note of his use of the first-person possessive.

"Too soon to say. But we'll need to keep a closer eye on global events. Poros made a tactical error. He gave Mateo Cardinale cause for revenge and exposed the nature of weapons under his control. The other cartels will see Poros as a threat. Expect reprisals, turf encroachments, and more scenes like this in the coming weeks."

I contained my giddiness. This savagery was a template for the chaos I envisioned on every planet after we cemented our empire. It also served as a reminder that we needed to tread with care.

"Understood, boss."

Elian's response was somewhat muted. I saw his fear. He'd all but given up on this planet, wanted to move everything off world. At least he referred to me with the proper respect that time.

"If this were all the news," I continued, "it would make for an ample breakfast. But another nugget arrived from the Sesquina Mountains. Judge Barron was found dead last night." I turned to Tracer. "You did a fine job. The investigators believe it was suicide. However, the cabin is being treated as a crime scene. No doubt they'll recover the evidence that will point to off-world interference.

"Until then, the Judge's death will stir the inevitable backlash and conspiracy theories in regard to the timing. That might motivate the insurrectionists to expedite their plans. If they do, we'll have to act sooner than later."

As I predicted, the President asked the UNF to look into the situation regarding Conquillos and the threat to its fifty-year lease. The head of Ground Operations agreed to send a delegation. When those folks arrived, pro-Aztecan tongues would be sure to wag; paranoia was certain to follow.

I had to admit: Working both sides against the middle was new to me. Destabilizing a planet produced many delightful conundrums. On the one hand, we were obliged to fulfill Ixoca's goal to raise the ire of the Aztecan people against the Collectorate. On the other, we prepared pro-Collectorate veterans to take down the insurrectionists as soon as they exposed themselves. I imagined the rest of the story would fall under the eventual heading "civil war."

As long as Black Star came out the other side intact (a few dozen casualties, but no more), I entertained every possibility. The key ingredient still missing from the grand picture: When Ixoca planned to call in his favor.

After our breaking news concluded, we moved on to the next stage of Black Star's evolution. Elian took the floor; his excitement returned in full flower. He tossed out the holos of each planetary report and started with G'hladi.

"This is the easy one. Our contacts can't wait for us to hit the ground running. These people are desperate."

111

He expanded an image of the primary production site, an abandoned processing center for poltash weed. The building was nondescript but twice as large as Desperido. It sat in the middle of barren brown fields that stretched more than a thousand hectares. Perhaps more obvious and exposed than we preferred. In this case, however, we didn't mind.

"The landowners are waiting for our signal," Elian continued. "They'll have the documents drawn up. We'll complete the buy within the first hour. Black Star will own an area almost as big as the Naugista Plateau."

Bett sighed. "I can't believe we're getting away with this. How much we stealing their land for?"

Elian didn't mind the pejorative.

"It's a goddamn steal, for sure. Five percent of its worth against the CCS price ten years ago. That was the last time they grew anything of value on the land. The sellers are highly motivated."

Indeed they were. G'hladi became legendary for centuries as home to the best poltash weed in the Collectorate. Nine years ago, a bacteria called craelix ruined most of the planet's poltash fields. It also fouled the soil for any other cash crops. Talk about a gut punch. We weren't the first off-worlders to take advantage of a desperate people, and damn well wouldn't be the last.

"How much are we laying out to hit full production?" She asked.

"We'll slide in under a half million, and that includes a startup pay stamp. The nearest town's on life support. Owners say there's about eight hundred working-age locals who are gonna treat us like gods. Ironic, huh? Motif will be coming off the line in two weeks."

Elian ran through the details, including the size and disposition of our army and which of his designers would manage the production. Though we expected no armed opposition, we'd have to install a large security blanket to cover so vast a territory. In some ways, we were about to create an independent state far from the probing eyes of any legitimate government.

112

That required manpower – in time, a third of our fighters. Eventually, we'd train the most loyal G'hladis to take over most of those roles; but that would require months, if not years. And what of all that useless land? Oh, Moon and I had plans which extended far beyond Motif production. A blank template of that size?

Gorgeous.

Next, Elian recapped a dicier proposition. We had formed an alliance with tribal elements in the thick jungles of Indonesia Prime, not far from the planet's famed Ularu Falls. It was nasty country – the bottom feeders of homo sapiens fled into those untamed lands. Their savagery was well-known. The indigenous tribes – direct descendants of the original colonists – spent generations trying to cleanse the land of those assholes.

The government never showed a desire to help. We did.

In exchange for our services to rid these tribes of the neighboring vermin, they set aside land for us and agreed to supply an ample workforce. The Wak'inau had many useful skills and produced their own line of natural hallucinogens. We agreed to distribute those alongside our own product.

Elian planned to land there in a week with four "extermination" teams. They'd join the Wak'inau to begin a thorough cleansing. Bett and Tracer had selected the forty most vicious and physically fit fighters for the job. We had yet to suffer casualties; I expected the first ones on Indonesia Prime.

In this regard, I gave Elian enormous credit. He intended to walk the jungle and help eradicate our new enemies. Sure, he'd fallen in love with good old-fashioned slaughter, but he had noble aims.

"If I'm gonna ask my people to risk their lives for my business, the least I can do is stand with them. It'll build loyalty, and loyalty is good for business."

OK, so some of it was profit-motivated. And yes, he'd taken to calling everyone in Desperido "my people," a sure sign of a budding narcissist. Eh. Takes one to know one. Yes?

113

At one point, I did casually bring up the notion that Elian might be tempting fate. He shrugged it off. Frankly, I never should've bothered. He wasn't yet thirty; thus, he expected to live forever. Ah, the foolishness of young humans. I remembered those times well.

We continued our discussions for the next hour, until the minutest of details were reviewed and approved. The G'hladi operation would begin the following day. Elian, Inky, and Genoa would lead the first wave onboard Maria, which was large enough to carry up to three overland chasers. We'd ferry the Scramjet between planets to deliver additional cargo. Worm travel meant we were never more than ninety minutes away. On day four, Elian's top designer Leia would take over the operation, and he would return here to prep for Indonesia Prime. Three days later, he would join Tracer and Moon in the killing jungles.

Some at our table were surprised I wasn't included in either expansion operation and that we didn't plan to use Bart in order to expedite fighters and equipment. Only Moon knew why, and he gave his blessing after much debate. To the others, I said obliquely:

"If we're not careful, we'll find ourselves caught in a maelstrom. My job is to make sure we navigate the proper course. That requires attention to certain items I alone must handle. Faith, my friends."

After the meeting closed, Moon and I stayed behind. Most of the table left the room before I said:

"Ship. May I have a moment of your time?"

The kid hung back. I asked him to sit.

Huh. Just the three of us. It almost felt like that first visit to Desperido. Quiet, lonely Desperido, where a boy with a metal arm provided two forcibly retired gods with an entry point to the new chapter in their lives.

"Yes, boss. What do you need? Have I done something wrong?"

He didn't have a clue. Good.

"Not at all, my friend. You remember our conversation on the way home from Conquillos. Yes?"

He leaned forward with a twinge of excitement.

"I do."

"Do you still wish to carry out your plans for Everdeen?"

"More than ever, boss. I done lots of thinking since we talked. Every time, I come to the same conclusion. It's something I got to finish."

Moon glared at me with a familiar, dour expression. He didn't like my upcoming answer one bit.

"Then I will take you there, Ship. Kill the assholes who betrayed you. Put that episode of your life forever behind."

Humans tended to behave quite differently when given permission to murder other people. Often, they responded with stern, somber expressions lending to the gravity of the affair. On occasion, I saw a twinkle in the eye that quietly said, "Oh, this is going to be so much fun!" Ship exhaled, as if finally unburdened of a dreadful weight.

He didn't understand what lay ahead. Or that I was bringing him along to kill three birds with a single stone.

I didn't tell them that three days earlier, Bart detected *Symphony New World* on deepstream. The Prez called us back to 40-Cignus. Her Security Chief Leonard would be expecting us. Or in this case, just me. I wanted Moon to stay here. In light of the new war between Cardinale and Poros, one of us needed to remain planetside at all times.

Yet even Moon did not know my third objective. I hated keeping secrets from my oldest friend, but he'd understand about this one.

Assuming it even worked.

Ship asked, "When do we go, boss?"

"Today. I'll advise your commanders. We'll arrive on Everdeen mid-morning local time."

The reality hit him upside the head like an overlooked two-by-four.

"Thank you, boss." He turned to Moon. "Thank you, boss."

"Too soon, my friend. Decide whether to be grateful after it's done. Have you chosen your weapons?"

"I have."

"Lovely. Meet me at Bart in six hours."

"Gotcha, boss."

He reached out to shake my hand, but I didn't budge.

"You're dismissed."

That wasn't awkward at all.

The instant we had the room to ourselves, Moon reached for his third cigar of the day.

"I see you didn't come to your goddamn senses, partner."

"Oh, please. The threat is minor, but the task is necessary."

He puffed on the newly-lit tobacco while shaking his head.

"Meeting Leonard. Yes. But Everdeen is a side mission. How many times have you said revenge never lives up to the billing?"

"Ship is rounding into form, my friend. The kid will not fulfill his potential until he sees the depth of his darkness."

Moon sat on the table's edge and glared at me between puffs.

"Or if he gets himself killed. Remember what Lumen said?"

"Absolutely. She was an aggravating coit, but she wasn't naïve. He may very well die on Everdeen, and I'd have to take the blame. I wasn't aware you cared about the kid."

He grunted like an ogre.

"No more than any of these humans. But we can't afford to lose fighters for no reason. And Ship? The army loves his spirit. If he dies, it'll hurt morale."

"Hurt, my friend. Not destroy. We have a full agenda packed with ample distractions. They'll be fine. Still wish to talk me out of it?"

"No."

Moon started for the door.

"Remember, Moon. You'll see it all through my eyes. I'll only be a whisper away."

He laughed. "So to speak."

I reached for the flask inside my jacket and contemplated the delicate maneuvers that might seal our fate.

13

WE TRAVELED THROUGH WORM for twenty minutes without a word from Ship. He sat in the co-pilot's chair and contemplated the murky netherworld of black substrata outside the forward viewport.

"Are you thinking of what you'll say before you kill them?"

The kid snapped out of his trance.

"Oh. Sorry, boss. What was that?"

He was laser-focused on something. A good sign, perhaps.

"Typically, Ship, I don't rehearse beforehand. I find an execution more satisfying when the words come naturally in the moment. Sometimes, I have the luxury of scouting my victims and learning their tendencies. Consequently, the parting message is context-appropriate. Do you know what you'll say to your victims?"

"N-no. I was thinking about my family. Will they recognize me after all this time?"

Huh. He was getting sentimental. Didn't care for that at all.

"Six years is a blip, my friend. You're taller, more muscular, and that weak mustache will be a surprise. Not to worry. Your mother will know at first sight. They always do. Don't fret about your family. They are not the targets."

He touched the mustache, a furry concoction he'd been trying to grow for six months.

"You think it's weak? Should I shave it off?"

Eh. Teenagers. The second-worst kind of humans.

"Kid, you're traveling three hundred light-years to murder people in cold blood. Don't concern yourself with facial hair."

"Yeah. You're right, boss." He unscrewed his flask and sipped. "I need to focus on what's important. It's just ... my family ... what if they refuse to tell me the names?"

"You'll make them."

"How?"

"You know how."

The kid dropped his head.

"No. I won't do that."

"Then you shouldn't be there. If they won't talk, shoot one of them. That's always a lovely motivator."

If this conversation went on much longer, Ship might've backed down. In theory, that would've improved his survival odds but got in the way of my larger plans.

"Don't worry about the difficult choices," I continued. "I'll be with you. Be glad you have a mentor. Wish I had one at your age."

"I'm sorry, boss. It's just ... I tried not to think about my family since I've been away. First, because they betrayed me. And then because it hurt too much."

"What hurt?"

He threw back a healthy dose of whiskey.

"When I was a little boy, I had the best life. Our home was right on the water. Me and my mates ... we spent so many days swimming and fishing ... I never had a worry."

"Happens to most children, Ship. It's called time's prison. A human poet wrote about it. *Time let me play and be golden in the mercy of his means, and green and golden I was huntsman and herdsman.* Do you know what that means?"

Ship stared at me like I was a stranger, which I found worthy of a chuckle.

"I'm very literate, my friend. Did you think I acquired my linguistic stylings through osmosis?"

"Dunno. You're a god."

"Was."

"I thought gods came by that stuff naturally."

Time for a drink.

"Talk to Moon often, do you?"

He forced a smile. "OK. I see your point, boss. Life was good back then because I didn't understand shit about the real world."

"Even now, you've barely scraped the surface. If you succeed on Everdeen, your eyes will open wider. Hard truths await beyond the gloaming. I had considerable blood on my hands before I knew what the universe planned for me."

"Which was what?"

"That I'd be a hero."

The kid lightened up.

"Guess the universe was right. You're my hero. A lot of other people say the same."

Oh, joy. A fan club. If only it was bigger, say to the tune of thirty-six billion.

"What I am, Ship, is a good salesman. The best. If you think of me as a hero, it's because I sold you on the idea. If someone makes a better case or I lead us to calamitous defeat, the label will disappear."

"Doubt that, boss. I'd follow you anywhere."

I went for the low-hanging fruit.

"Even into fire?"

"Every time."

"Huh. Excellent. Because where we're headed, fire is inevitable. That's why you cannot hesitate today. If you intend to see this through, close your heart. Shut off your cudfrucking emotions and find the targets, no matter the consequence to others. Understand?"

In typical fashion of a teen boy trying to impress, Ship bucked up his shoulders, steeled his jaw, and breathed imaginary fire.

"I will, boss. I promise."

"Good. I'm out of advice on that topic. What say we change the subject? Yes?"

"Sure, boss. What do you wanna talk about?"

"I'm more interested in what's on your mind. Do you have any questions about our future operations? Our off-world expansion?"

He pondered for a bit before snapping his fingers.

"Oh, yes. I know! So, I was drinking with some of the fellas in my unit last night. They wondered why you chose Indonesia Prime for a new facility. Actually, it wasn't so much the planet as the location. They said the stories about those jungles near Ularu were legendary. Horrible things happened there. And they said it was very hot and humid. All year."

"Ah. Were they complaining?"

"No, boss. Just curious. They thought I might know since I'm on the table of trust."

"What did you tell them?"

"Just that we struck a deal with the Wak'inau and they agreed to work for us. I don't think I ever heard you or Ilan or Elian explain why you chose that place."

"It's a fascinating topic, kid."

This seemed like a great opportunity to open the door to one of those elusive truths Ship would have to face sooner than later.

"Tell me, Ship. You spent three days at the facility on Inuit Kingdom. What did you observe about the locals?"

"Observe?"

"What impression did they make?"

The kid shrugged.

"Dunno. I mean, not much. They were quiet, followed orders, worked hard."

"Would you say they were grateful for the work?"

"Oh, yes. No one was ever late to a shift. Elian said they worked their asses off." Ship laughed. "Nothing but glitter, he said."

"Did you observe their living conditions?"

Those eyes ballooned. He understand where I was headed.

"The towns were poor. They didn't have much."

"Exactly. The same can be said of the mountains of Bolivar, the poltash fields of G'hladi, and the jungles of Indonesia Prime. Our pattern follows a tried and true human tradition. We find the hopeless and the forgotten. The people who subsist on meager portions. We give them a better life, and they return the favor with hard work and abject loyalty. It's called exploitation, my friend.

"Every expert criminal enterprise with an eye toward global or interstellar aspirations has always known two things. One, avoid the light of an urban setting, where threats from competition and law enforcement are legion. Two, use people who will easily sacrifice morality in exchange for survival. That begins with humans in need of food and quality shelter. The rest is negotiable."

He studied me like a student who'd just been smacked with a grand revelation about life. Yet he needed time to process it.

"So, that's how we'll build our empire?"

"Yes, my friend. On the backs of the dispossessed, disaffected, and disgusted. They were never invited to join proper society, so they have no problem living outside its laws. And you'd be amazed how many fit the label. We will never run short of recruits."

Ship mulled my explanation with a cautious grin.

"So, we'll be heroes to these people."

I gave him credit: The kid knew how to look on the bright side.

"Hero worship is a flimsy foundation on which to form a business. Foremost, we're their employers. Yes, they'll be paid a fair wage and their lives will improve. But they'll also do as they're told. Anyone who goes rogue or outright defies us will be killed."

The kid bristled at the whole truth.

"Each body will be cremated, my friend, and replaced by someone of equal desperation. Black Star is no charity and abides by no labor laws. You will be well served to remember. Someday, you might find yourself running a facility."

"Sure, boss. You, uh, you think I'll make for a good manager?"

"Many bridges to cross before then." I studied the worm drive tracker. "We're thirty seconds from the exit aperture. Time for a little intrigue."

Ship tightened his eyebrows.

"Wait, what? We can't be at Everdeen already."

"We aren't. Ship, there's a matter I must see to before we deal with your family reunion. You've often asked how Ilan and I receive information about our next assassination."

"And you always say it's too soon for me to know."

I chuckled.

"Not anymore, kid. Hold tight."

On cue, the sun-bright aperture swirled around us, accompanied by the familiar thunder. Bart buckled through the turbulence then emerged into open space.

"Where are we, boss?"

"40-Cignus. Its star went nova ninety thousand years ago."

His eyes twinkled when he beheld the gaseous remains. They painted a nice backdrop of red and violet.

"Never heard of this system. Is it inside the Collectorate?"

"Outer reaches of the sector. Nothing of scientific value here, and it's off the primary shipping routes, which is why we chose it." I tilted the Nav holo toward Ship. "This, my friend, is our destination. Twenty kilometers ahead. The asteroid has no name, but it contains the drop."

"Very nice, boss. So, your client leaves the mission details there."

"Afterward, we provide proof of a job well done. Today, however, will be different. The exchange of information will be a bit more intimate. So to speak."

I jumped from the Nav chair and told Ship to take the controls.

"Bart will bring us in on a programmed track. Normally, we touch down. Today, we'll hover. Enact the searchlights at one kilometer out."

"Yeah. Sure, boss. What are you ...?" He saw me open the EV storage. "That makes sense. Got to breathe out there."

"Actually, I don't. My syneth remains stable for thirty-four minutes in a vacuum. Used to be seventeen, but we tested it recently. Ilan and I are much more flexible after merging with Ixoca."

However, I didn't need my expected guest to know that. Better I showed a human vulnerability.

I hadn't worn an EV suit in ages, but memory served me well. I slipped into it like an old pro but wondered why, after two millennia in space, humans hadn't found a lighter, more efficient alternative.

Huh.

The answer likely existed somewhere in my syneth matrix. Create a successful prototype, and I'd have a legitimate business opportunity.

Nice.

When Bart moved into position several meters from the drop, I gave Ship new orders.

"Catalyze the worm drive. Reset the coordinates for the location labelled Backstop. Spool her up for a sudden exit."

Ship didn't touch a thing, though he had mastered the drive.

"Wait, boss. What's going on? Where is Backstop?"

"The far end of the system. Close enough to monitor local activity in case of an emergency."

"Like?"

I slogged about in that awkward suit but remained near the egress.

"Here's hoping you never know, my friend. Set the drive. If you hear me say 'stage right,' open an aperture."

"Then what?"

"Wait for new instructions, of course. No worries. Ilan is watching.

He knows the plan."

I pressed the printlock beside the egress. A cascade barrier spread across the bulwark to prevent decompression when the egress opened.

"Enjoy the show, kid."

I leaped out and proceeded toward the drop, an open pom in my right hand. It connected to Bart's Nav and surveillance systems. It saw no sign of other ships after we exited worm, but the President's people could've left behind a whole array of goodies. Unfortunately, the last few days watching events through Kai Parke's eyes offered no clue as to what.

The President's Chief of Staff currently slept in his nice warm bed at Amity Station. Unless the Prez gave her Security Chief Leonard new orders, I expected him to be waiting in the local stellar neighborhood. Our arrival undoubtedly set off a beacon. That gave me a minute or two to contemplate the next step.

"Ship," I said inside the kid's mind. "I've been remiss in your training. Next time we go out together, remind me to suit you up for a some EV action."

"That would be f-fun, boss."

He didn't say it like he meant it.

I scanned the drop's titanium casement and detected no potential obstacles. It opened without exploding in my face, which was a positive development.

That's because there was nothing inside. Not even a memglass.

OK, then.

At the very least, Leonard should have offered me a distraction. What did he expect me to do? Count the stars?

Ship's voice rang out:

"Bart's worm tracker. It's detecting ..."

"Yes, yes. Thanks, my friend. I see it."

Wormhole trackers were relatively new tech, invented by the Aeternans more than twenty years ago. They kept commercial shipping well-regulated and made life interesting for smugglers and other ne'er-do-wells. However, their range was limited to roughly half a billion kilometers.

Rogue elements like me weren't supposed to have access.

Eh. Naïve humans.

Right on schedule, a new star exploded near the asteroid. The flare vanished right after a dark silhouette passed through. I turned up my optical sensors and made out the ship's running lights.

Oh, well. Time to play nice.

I opened a channel.

"Hello there. Is that you, Leonard?"

I received no reply, but the vessel's searchlights came alive.

"I'll take that as a yes."

The President's Security Chief seemed a tad irked.

"You sound as if you expected me. How?"

No point giving away my tactical advantage.

"I didn't, but who else knows about this place, my friend? You sent the signal, yet there's nothing in the casement. You wouldn't be trying to trap me out here, by chance?"

"No. We need to talk. Is your partner with you?"

I didn't want to get too flippant with the man. However …

"Sorry. He's busy today. Big galaxy, much to do."

"Who's inside your ship?"

"No threat to you, Leonard. Now, why don't you join me out here? Let's chat."

14

SECURITY FELLAS ARE PARANOID by nature. It's a quality skillset if you happen to be protecting the most powerful human for nine hundred light-years. Leonard took his time agreeing to an EV confab. He conceded only after I threatened to leave.

Ah, what a moment. Face to face, no more than six feet apart. The internal helmet lamps illuminated our faces.

"So, my friend, you came a long way for an audience. Are you here on behalf of the President or yourself?"

Leonard struck me as one of those guys who shifted between two expressions: Stone-faced and rock-faced. Another skillset of a security professional?

"We have questions. Answer them honestly, or our association terminates today."

"Oh. Well. That sounds ominous. Is the President unsatisfied with our work?"

"You eliminated every target."

I heard a caveat inside the compliment.

"We're the best, Leonard."

"Her conditions were specific from the first day: No collateral damage. Do you remember?"

"I do, my friend. It was a very stressful time for both of us. She didn't want to see me, but I gave her little choice. And you, Leonard? You kept your distance. I'm sure you were following orders."

Nothing in the man's eyes betrayed the moment.

"You were paid to kill one man on Qasi Ransome. You murdered more than two hundred fifty."

"Old news. And we've worked for you twice since then, so the misfortunes of bystanders must not have weighed too heavily on anyone's conscience."

"I'm not here to discuss morality. The President has questions about your recent actions."

None of this came as a surprise, of course. I feigned ignorance.

"Oh, really? We stamped out quite a problem on Azteca. Did we do something wrong?"

"You're pursuing a different agenda. You were paid to kill Anton Cherry and Reynaldo Barron. That should have been the end of it. Instead, you forced a regional governor to resign and killed Maris Sylva, one of the most influential corporate leaders."

"We did, Leonard. They belonged to the Q6 conspiracy. More bang for your buck."

Leonard balled his fists together, as much as one could in an EV suit. Still, it was the first sign of an emotional response.

"Sylva contacted the UNF about just such a conspiracy in the hour before she died. The governor was replaced by someone sympathetic to our interests. And Judge Barron miraculously did an about-face on his legal positions the same day he died. Now, our latest intel suggests the evidence of his death points to SI. Not the suicide you arranged. You orchestrated these events."

"Ah. You want to know our game."

"The President does not pay you to take initiative or go beyond the mission parameters."

"Yet we do it for no extra charge, Leonard. Given the incident shortly after Qasi Ransome, I'd say we're behaving with great

128

restraint. In fact, it's quite remarkable we continue to work for you at all."

Leonard narrowed his eyes.

"What incident?"

"You know, my friend. The Fort of Inarra. Our previous home, wiped clean from the face of Azteca."

Surely, he expected the topic to arise.

"*That.* Yes. We heard. At first, we assumed you both died."

"Naturally. That was the goal, after all."

"You think we tried to have you killed."

"You deny it?"

"I do."

"Ah. I see. Our tiny home is obliterated by an unconstitutional attack on a sovereign world, and the only people who knew we lived there simply shrug their shoulders. You see why I might be skeptical of your denial."

Moon and I knew the orders came down through the President's office. The night we met Ixoca, his many eyes took us inside a meeting where Leonard, President Aleksanyan, and Chief of Staff Kai Parke discussed our next potential job. Ixoca then switched focus to a ship where its Captain gave orders to bomb the Fort of Inarra. That same Captain, utterly irate after the fort's security system fried his ground team, said, "He will pay for this."

We never heard the Captain's name or knew whether he referred to Leonard or Kai. Not that it mattered. We saw the event play out through the Captain's eyes, which meant he was either one of Ixoca's generals or passive observers. We heard three officers mentioned by name: Col. Raeger, Lt. Suh, and Commander Turin. Just enough intel to begin discreet research.

"Yes," Leonard said. "We debated your fate, but the President needed your continued services. We did not order an attack on your home. She's grateful you survived."

"Is she? How lovely. The President is an impressive woman. When

I knew her simply as Kara, we helped each other through a perilous time. Only a few days, mind you, and it didn't end well. But she struck me as a passionate coit. She had no fear of men in high places. I wasn't surprised when she rose to power."

I detected his impatience. Eh. Might as well get to it.

"Leonard, my partner and I decided long ago to forgive the error in judgment. We wrote off Inarra as a miscalculation. When you called us back into service, we knew whoever gave the order now regretted it. That's why we continued to work for the President. However, you must understand: For us, this is a parttime gig. We're building a business on the side. I'm quite sure your agents have made you aware.

"Now, if our separate agenda concerns the President, we'll agree to terminate the relationship after we receive payment for taking out Cherry and Barron. Thoughts, my friend?"

Did he expect so much transparency? In his shoes, I might've been a bit thrown off my game.

"What is your business? Will it work against the President's agenda?"

"Which is what, my friend?"

"Peace. Unity. Order."

Naturally, I had to chuckle.

"Only that, you say? Literally, the three hardest things for humans to maintain. No worries, Leonard. Our business will never clash with President Aleksanyan's ambitious agenda."

I could've added that she'd be assassinated before our brand of chaos entered the galactic marketplace. I calculated she had less than three months to live.

"What is the nature of your business?"

"You don't want to know, Leonard. Neither does she."

"Night market? Drugs? Weapons?"

"Business, my friend. Leave it alone."

He didn't. Asshole.

"In the last few weeks, we've heard reports of a mercenary group called Black Star. What do you know of it?"

Nice. We were building a rep inside the intelligence community. But *mercenary*? Those amateur outfits never amounted to squat. I fought off the impulse to take offense.

"I know nothing about Black Star, but it is a swell name. Leonard, I'm not going to discuss our outside ventures. We did the President an enormous solid on Azteca. We're due payment. Deposit the funds, and we'll await the next assignment. What else is there to discuss, my friend?"

"I am not your friend. Neither is the President."

"True. We'll never sit down for a nice Kohlna steak and a glass of white wine. But we do have a mutually beneficial relationship. And I'm sure you counseled her from the start to avoid this path."

He nodded. "I did."

"You don't trust us. Understandable. But luring us out here under false pretenses hardly engenders our trust, either. So, you have all the answers you'll receive today. Go back to her. Decide whether our relationship continues. If yes, send the signal for our next job. If no, submit payment minus one credit. We'll accept the verdict."

I didn't expect Leonard to concede quickly, but what choice could a wise man make? If he did in fact have a ship hiding in near space preparing to jump out of worm and obliterate us, he dared not call in the strike. Moon wasn't here. Leonard knew better than to leave one of us alive and filled with rage. Yet he needed to save face.

"You'll receive payment within a standard day." Leonard roughened his tone. "In full! If the President changes her mind about you, then her silence will be the verdict."

"I see. Don't call us; we'll call you. Yes?"

Apparently, he decided not to dignify my remark with a response. Leonard retreated to his ship.

"Until the next job, my friend," I said before cutting the channel.

I almost ordered Ship to activate Bart's forward guns, just to screw with Leonard. He'd no doubt recommend the President cut ties before we became too much of a liability. Then she'd politely decline. Too much at stake, she'd say. Too many forces threatening our peace, unity, and order.

She tried hard. I admired that quality. Alas, this Collectorate would not have the staying power of its predecessor. The Chancellors ruled for a thousand years by fiat and the largest military ever assembled. Kara had neither resource.

Leonard's ship opened an aperture and disappeared inside. No parting words. Huh.

However, I heard quite a few words and saw a jaw hanging limp when I entered Bart and closed the egress.

Ship waited in the center of the bay.

"The President? You kill people for President Aleksanyan?"

Didn't even give me time to remove that awful EV suit.

"Don't act shocked, kid. I told you the President and I went back a ways. And you knew I worked for very important people. Simple deductive reasoning should've taken you all the way home."

"But boss. She's the President. Does she pay other assassins?"

"Never asked. And she doesn't pay me directly. That would be a career-killer. No, she follows the same procedure as everyone at the top of the food chain. The credits cannot be traced back to her."

I stowed the suit.

"Ship, you were the first Aztecan to learn I wasn't human. Why? Because I trusted you."

An exaggeration, but it made him feel good.

"So, I thought it appropriate you be the first to know the identity of my client." I slipped into the Nav chair and reached for my flask. "Your reaction is why Ilan and I chose to conceal the information. Imagine what would happen if this became common knowledge in Desperido."

The kid cursed under his breath.

"A secret this big? A lot of them wouldn't trust you anymore."

"Correct. It would raise too many questions we're not yet prepared to answer. Someone looking to make a name for himself might use the knowledge to betray us."

Ship nodded sharply as he accepted my rationale.

"Can I ask another question?"

"You can try."

"Those business trips you talked about, the ones to other planets. Were they ...?"

I grinned. "Most."

"How long have you ...?"

"Two years plus change."

"If I tell anyone about what I know ..."

"I'll shoot you in the head."

Ship grabbed his flask with a trembling hand.

"Gotcha, boss. I-I'm good. Won't say a word."

"Why are you so jittery, my friend?"

"Dunno. I mean, you're right. I shouldn't be so shocked. I knew you were a killer, right from the start. That didn't stop me from wanting to be just like you."

The compliment warmed my so-called heart.

"Look at today's revelation for what it truly is: Proof that you are learning from the best."

He cracked a smile. Progress.

"That's true. The President wouldn't hire just anybody."

"Very good. Now, time to resume our journey. Next stop: Everdeen. Twenty-nine minutes to go. Reset the worm drive to our previous course. Take us out, Ship."

Like any kid, he loved being handed responsibility.

"Gotcha, boss. Redirecting to Everdeen."

After we entered the aperture and verified the course settings, I lowered my seatback and closed my eyes.

"I'll leave you to the controls and to contemplate what lies ahead. I intend to take a short nap. Wake me at two minutes out."

"On it, boss."

I didn't nap. Instead, I reassessed my encounter with Leonard. Were my instincts about his answers correct? Did he prove an unspoken theory I developed months ago regarding the destruction of our fort?

If the President had ordered the attack and knew it failed, why reengage with us for additional jobs? Why lure us out here only to ask a few questions about logistical concerns? Leonard would not have mentioned Black Star unless he knew who ran it. Which meant he also knew where we lived. And, quite possibly, the size and disposition of our little army.

They could have hit us at any time. Sure, taking out an entire town would have raised questions but also eliminated a pair of loose, dangerous threads.

Yeah, no. The President wanted us alive. She might have entered the deal reluctantly, but our work became indispensable. Humans who taste absolute power never want to let go. They morph into creatures once considered reprehensible. All actions are justified.

She never gave the order. I knew that now. Leonard had the means but not the will; he'd never defy her.

Which brought me to Kai Parke, the Chief of Staff. He carried a piece of Ixoca. Like Leonard, his loyalty was absolute. After four months of observation, I never saw anything to suggest a personal agenda.

Yet someone gave the order. My research pulled together enough visual threads to conclude the attacking ship belonged to SI. Col. Raeger and Cdr. Turin were retired UNF officers now listed as independent contractors on their respective home worlds. I found nothing on Lt. Suh. And the Captain who led the mission? Not only did I never learn his name, but a thorough search of Ixoca's many eyes failed to find him. Which meant he died soon afterward or ...

As Elian would say: Nothing but glitter!

I loved moments of revelation. They never let me down.

It was time to take action.

That's where Everdeen came into play. Sure, the kid could have his fun. Seek his revenge. We weren't actually going there for him.

I had much more important work to do.

15

ON THE FACE OF IT, Henniford Island was a tropical goddamn paradise. Gently swaying palms, a crisp breeze off the sea, and flowers, flowers everywhere. Folks wore bright colors under wide, floppy hats and greeted each other with pearly smiles. Huh. Were these Caribs genuinely pleased to meet us, or was their behavior ingrained for generations? Was this how they used to greet 'special clients?'

Oh, the official line said no one here had engaged in The Trade since the People's Collectorate outlawed it in 5368. Official lines rarely resembled the truth. Ship's experience confirmed as much.

We left Bart in a public parking lodge built upon a former UNF training center. Ship led the way through the adjoining town. Its narrow cobblestone streets lent a quaint historical value that the Caribs advertised to off-world tourists. My research said they aimed marketing campaigns at a wealthy, youthful demographic. In other words, those too young to care about its sordid history.

Judging from the sparse foot traffic and vacant shops, the effort did not appear successful. Perhaps we caught them on an off-day.

I was not sympathetic. These people thrived under the first Collectorate; the Chancellors looked the other way while taking a healthy percentage of the profits.

Yes, I did awful things to humans – primarily, killing them in large numbers – but I drew the line at sexual torture. Especially in regard to children. Historians estimated more than five million were forced into service over three hundred years. Some as young as five. I knew one. Though he survived and flourished, many did not.

Why did it bother me so? After all, the galaxy I hoped to create would stand as a lasting testament to savagery and despair. As we strolled down the main street of Henniford Town, the answer became clear. These assholes and their ancestors denied children the chance to become time's prisoners. To experience a few years of bliss, free from the brutal journey ahead.

However, I was not the avenging angel today. That job fell upon Ship, who maintained an admirable composure. He carried a pistol, blast rifle, and a knife beneath his beige jacket. He blended in well, as did I. Before we exited Bart, I shapeshifted into an older Carib with a spritz of gray hair and a scraggly beard. I wore a white shirt with a sheer fabric and smoked poltash weed from a small black pipe.

"Strange to be home, my friend?"

Ship didn't take his eye off the colorful shops from which playful music emanated.

"This ain't my home. Nothing looks like I remember."

"You're taller and older now. The town shrunk."

He nodded. "Yes, boss. That's what I was thinking. It don't seem as grand as before."

"How far to your home?"

"A few blocks."

"What's my name?"

"Jean Mathis."

"Good. Do I sound Carib?"

"Oh, yes, boss. Spot on."

Shapeshifting from a template wasn't difficult. Dialects, however, did not come with the genetic package and often required practice. Six months with Ship aided my cause. Jean Mathis was a wizened old fool who never amounted to much growing up on the mainland but found success in the smuggling arena. Rather than participate in The Trade, he rescued victims before they reached their destination among these islands. That was my story, if anyone asked.

Ship froze when he spotted his home at the end of a long street bordering the waterfront. It rose on stilts, beneath which lay a pair of rowboats and a vast array of fishing nets. I had imagined a sprawling estate, not a home clustered among so many. Almost every house we passed had a small chicken coop out front. I turned down my olfactory sensors.

"One step forward, kid. Then the other. Time for your big reveal."

He stopped at the base of tall wooden stairs.

"They took me out in the middle of the night, boss. They taped my mouth shut and warned me not to make a sound. An hour later, I left Everdeen on a transport. My hands and legs were bound. The smugglers paid me little mind."

I tried not to make light of the boy's plight.

"The night market is not known for its accommodations. Comfy seats with headrests and meal service are rarely included."

"My family threw me away like trash."

Ship tapped into his rage a little soon for my taste.

"They're not the targets, my friend. Smile. Maintain composure. You need them."

I rested a hand on his shoulder. The kid trembled with fear and anger in equal doses.

"Sorry, boss. I rehearsed this moment. Thought I was ready."

Footsteps approached from behind. A lilting female voice said:

"What might I do for you, sirs?"

The woman carried a large basket of fruits tucked against her ample chest. I saw the resemblance straightaway. When her eyes fell on Ship, she revealed nothing but terror.

"Mother."

She lost her grip on the basket. A fruit stand fell at our feet.

Before she collapsed, I grabbed hold of her.

"Whoa, there. I have you." I chuckled and told Ship, "As I said, the mother always knows."

She caught her breath.

"Mende?"

"Yes, Mother. It's me."

"How ...? It can't ... you shouldn't be here."

Not the greeting I predicted after six years. Where was the tear-soaked hug and the hallelujah?

Eh. So much for lofty expectations.

"Don't worry, Mother. I won't stay long. Oh, and never call me that name again. I go by Ship Foster now. Mende is no more."

Nice recovery. The kid regained his poise.

"What? Mende ..."

"Ship."

"We never knew what happened to you. Why are you here?"

"A long story, but not one for the street. We must go inside."

She began collecting the spilled fruit. I offered to help.

"We apologize for the shock," I told her. "My name is Jean Mathis. I am Ship's benefactor." I grabbed the full basket. "Allow me."

Searching for my trademark dulcet tone was a tad trickier using the local Carib dialect.

"Do I have the pleasure of meeting Mrs. Mariel Sutton?"

She swallowed an egg while looking past us in obvious fear.

"I am."

"Excellent. Perhaps if we could speak in a private setting?"

Before she answered, Ship added:

"Who else is home, Mother?"

"Y-your brother Benjamin."

Not everyone Ship hoped to question, but the limited inventory would have to do on such short notice. We followed her to the top of the steps before Ship asked the next logical question.

"Where is Father?"

139

Her eyes glazed over.

"He passed four years ago."

Ship didn't miss a beat.

"How?"

"A fishing accident. He drowned."

Not a sign of grief in his demeanor. Quick acceptance. Outstanding.

"Please, wait here, Son. I must prepare your brother."

She disappeared inside.

"Prepare him?" I asked. "Why?"

"Benjamin and I were very close. He felt betrayed when I protested about our family's involvement in The Trade. He beat me to an inch of my life."

"Huh. That's new. So, losing the arm wasn't your only physical punishment. I'm sorry, Ship."

He smirked. "Benjamin was a coward. And he doesn't need time to prepare. C'mon."

We entered a brightly-lit home with large windows which allowed in the breeze. The place was well-apportioned in vibrant colors and smelled of tropical flowers. Positively delightful. How utterly ironic.

Ship led me through the kitchen and into a large living space, where we landed upon the other resident.

Benjamin rose from a couch wearing only water trunks. He was two years older than Ship but bore little resemblance. Perhaps it was the obesity or the bloodshot eyes. Or the bone necklace.

"I told you to wait outside," Mrs. Sutton said.

"You don't give me orders anymore. Hello, Benjamin."

"Mende?"

"Ship. My name is Ship."

Benjamin didn't care. He balled his fists. The asshole appeared ready to have at it again.

"Leave! We will lose everything if they know you are here."

He moved toward us with his chest pumped out in a menacing

posture. He intended to show us the door.

Yeah, no.

Mother Sutton restrained him.

"Benjamin, settle yourself. He is your brother."

"Why? Why is he here?"

I thought to intervene. No one had a beef with me.

"Might I suggest we sit and discuss the matter?"

The room did not fill with appreciation and conciliation.

"Who the fuck is this man?" Benjamin shouted.

"I'm your brother's advocate. If you would hear him out ..."

"Not a word. He leaves now."

Mrs. Sutton finally displayed a few tears.

"Son, please. Calm yourself. He does not intend to stay."

"I don't want to hear it. We been through enough, Mother."

Ship did not move a muscle until Benjamin pushed their mother aside. Then my young apprentice popped open a button in his jacket, reached inside, and grabbed a pistol, which he aimed between his brother's eyes.

"You will listen to me, Benjamin. You and Mother will sit and listen. And you will answer my questions. If you do not, I will kill you where you stand."

Now that's what I called a family reunion! Ship had never spoken with the tone of a demanding bully. Just psychotic enough to be credible. Nice.

Benjamin played tough guy for his mother.

"You won't dare, Mende."

"I have killed many men, Brother. You will be one more."

Amid their understandable paralysis at this dramatic change from the child they once knew, Benjamin and his mother glanced my way. Did they expect me to calm Ship? Oh, OK.

"I recommend you follow instructions, my friends. Ship is quite efficient. A true professional, if you get my meaning."

They did. Couch time.

Ship circled around and plopped into a chair, his trigger hand resting comfortably on the armrest. He stared at them with outward disdain, but I suspected he had hoped for a warmer reception.

"Where is my brother Aaron?"

"No business of yours, Mende."

This Benjamin character was begging for pain. His mother interceded just in time.

"Be quiet, Son. Aaron does not live here any longer. He married two years ago. He moved off the island."

"And Renetta?"

"She is at work. Renetta has a job in the governor's office."

Mother Sutton didn't say it with pride.

"What?" Ship laughed. "Renetta hated government. All she wanted to be was a dancer."

She looked away. "Things change."

Ship narrowed his eyes on Benjamin.

"What about you? Are you still good for anything, Brother?"

I had warned Ship not to become antagonistic. He needed answers from these people.

"Ship, my friend. I'm sure Benjamin does a fine job looking after your mother. Perhaps if we take a step back. Yes?"

"No, Jean. They ruined my life. I owe them nothing."

Benjamin took the bait. Dumbass.

"You brought it on yourself, Mende."

He aimed the weapon toward Benjamin's privates.

"Call me that name again, and you will never fuck anyone."

Yep. I'd say four months in the company of ex-military had done wonders for Ship's aggressive tendencies.

"Boys, please!" Mother Sutton broke into a steady stream of tears. "Enough. Ship, please lower the gun. It does not have to be this way. We are so very sorry. We had no choice, you see."

Ship abided by the request.

"About what? Cutting off my arm? Beating the ten hells out of me?

Sending me off-world, not caring what happened?"

"Please. Please. You knew the tradition. I warned you not to speak up. If you had only held your peace."

"I was your youngest child. You and Father did not even try to protect me. My own brother almost killed me. After Father cut off my arm, you fitted me with a metal claw."

She leaned into Benjamin, who hugged her.

"We cannot change what happened, Son. I see you have a very good prosthetic. I am happy for you."

Ship gave me the side-eye, so I stepped in.

"Oh, yes. Only the best for Ship. The arm set me back a great deal, but your son earned it. He helped me at a critical juncture in my life, and I responded in kind."

"Who are you to him?" Benjamin asked.

"Jean Mathis. Commodities dealer. I conduct my business off the usual trails."

"Night market. You are a smuggler."

As if he had cause to be judgmental.

"Better, my friend. I make dreams come true for people who have been mistreated. I advised against his return to Everdeen. But Ship has grown into an independent-minded young assassin. He believes in resolving the past to chart a better future."

They homed in on one word, of course.

"Assassin?" Benjamin stammered.

"No, please, Son. You will not hurt us."

I'd never seen Ship look so in command; although in fairness, an amateur could've finished the job. They sat slightly outside point-blank.

"I can never forgive the things you did to me. My love for this family washed away years ago. When I have what I came for, I will leave this planet and never return. If you are lucky, I will not kill you."

Firm but reasonable, all things considered.

"What is it you want from us, Son?"

"Names."

"Of whom?"

"I know the truth about what happened that night. You and Father did not banish me from Everdeen. You sent me away because others were planning to kill me as retribution."

Mother Sutton wiped her tears and nodded.

"Yes. Yes, Son. We had no choice, you see. Like I said before. We saved your life."

"Did you know about it, Brother?"

Benjamin cleared his throat.

"Not until the next day."

"You're lying, but I don't care. I want the names of the people who ordered my death."

Mother and Son shared a terrified glance and shook their heads.

"Why, Ship?" She asked. "Why does it matter?"

"I want the names."

"What will you do if we tell you, Brother?"

"I intend to kill them."

That was their least favorite answer. She screwed her eyes as if Ship had gone mad (which, for the moment, he had). Benjamin laughed, but not the kind meant to mock.

"Have you lost your mind?" Benjamin turned to me. "Talk sense into him. You two must leave here while you can."

"Oh, now. Ship is a man on a mission. It's not my place."

The kid decided to build on the theater. He opened the left side of his jacket to reveal a blast rifle strapped to the lining.

"I'm going to kill them. What are their names?"

Mother Sutton grabbed her chest and feigned a heart attack.

"What has become of you, Son? What kind of man are you?"

Ship closed his jacket.

"A man who will never be pushed around again. You will tell me who these people are and where I can find them."

144

Benjamin held his mother's hand and calmed her.

"Ship. Please, Brother. Listen to me. The people you seek are too powerful. They will kill you."

"Leave that shit to me to worry about, Brother."

"No. You misunderstand. After they kill you, they will come for all of us. Your entire family."

Ship raised a mischievous smile.

"Not if I kill every last goddamn one of them."

"No, Son. We will not do this. We cannot. Aaron has two babies. Renetta has a girl five years old. No. We will not help you."

So there it was. The inevitable stalemate. Ship and I talked about this moment a great deal. I counseled shooting someone, but only after a fair bit of negotiation.

"A question, if I might, friends? Are you expecting visitors in the next, say, two hours?"

They studied each other for an agreeable answer. Mother said:

"No. Renetta will not be coming home for luncheon today. No one."

"Excellent. Ship, might I suggest you use the time to catch up on the past. Your Mother and Brother are obviously shocked and their minds in utter disarray. Pull back from the brink. Give them time to reconsider your request."

Ship agreed with my strategy.

"If time runs out and I don't have an answer, I'm going to shoot you, Brother. You'll die in Mother's arms. It's fitting. You were always her favorite."

Ouch. *Estranged* didn't begin to describe the dynamic.

"I'm in the way, my friends." I glanced outside past the balcony. "I see you have a lovely dock. I'll walk out there and give you time to sort through your concerns. Good, Ship?"

"Yeah, Jean. I got this."

He grew up so quickly. If I were his dad, perhaps a tear would've been in order. I bid farewell and left the awkward scene in limbo.

145

Time to deal with more important business.

16

SHIP PUT ON A FINE SHOW, but he'd yet to prove he could see it through. The kid faced an especially trying decision; best he make it without my influence.

That was my excuse for leaving him alone with his family. I too had a crucial choice to consider, one which I delayed for much longer than predicted. The end of the Suttons' lonely dock felt like the perfect spot.

An artist might have set his easel here and captured the beauty that masked the truth about this place. The placid water was emerald green and crystal clear. Rowboats and sloops moved between Henniford and the nearest two islands, only a few kilometers away. A flock of pink seabirds flew overhead.

Lovely.

I strove for chaos among humans, not nature. I respected it far too much.

With my butt planted on the dock and my feet dangling over the edge, I leaned forward and studied my reflection. The wise old Carib stared back. These were my only eyes.

The others had begun to blur sometime during the journey from 40-Cignus. What were once hundreds of perspectives across many worlds gradually faded. As they went blind, so too did the hearing.

The last one disappeared two hundred light-years from Azteca.

I couldn't even see inside the Sutton living room.

As I suspected, Ixoca could only extend his many eyes but so far. He claimed that his three thousand terraform shafts, configured as a global network, transmitted and received the pieces of his heart across the entire sector.

Yeah, no.

I spent the first few weeks after the merger mapping the locations of his many eyes. Three-fourths resided in the Aztecan system. The farthest? A hundred thirty light-years away. That by itself did not counter the Jewel's claim. He simply had less resources elsewhere. Fortunately, the President's office on Amity Station resided seventy light-years out.

Time to know for certain if I was right about him.

"Ixoca? We have an important matter to discuss."

Typically, the Jewel's presence felt as normal as a steady heartbeat. He was easy to take for granted. When his emotions rose or his voice entered my mind, the pulse elevated. While I conversed with Ixoca, the so-called heartbeat raced and my syneth matrix energized.

That dynamic changed in the final leg of today's journey. At first, I wondered if the deadened sensation was a product of wormhole travel. Would the heartbeat return in normal space?

"Ixoca? Are you there? We need to talk, my friend."

Nothing. No pulse. No energized syneth.

Me. Alone.

For the first time in four months.

Nice.

I closed my eyes and leaped inside my mind, burrowing through my human consciousness and poking around in the deep, hidden corners of my syneth matrix. I dug into holes so tiny, dark and claustrophobic, I would lose my sanity if trapped there for long. They went ignored when Moon and I were *maximos deos*, for they served no apparent purpose. What intelligence could survive there and have any hope of finding its way to the surface?

Fortunately, I knew of one.

"Hello, my friend. We can speak now."

A familiar itching sensation crawled forth from a dark, hopeless tunnel. And then a voice.

"What took you so long?"

"My apologies, Theo. I had hoped to make contact sooner, but circumstance prevented it."

A long wail echoed through that tunnel. Was it Theo or the part of Addis he inherited?

"You don't know what it's been like for us."

"It can't have been more painful than inserting pieces of yourself into human data systems."

"There are different kinds of pain, Royal. Loneliness. Isolation. Desperation."

I could've reminded Theo he was centuries old and often went years without having a meaningful role in my life. That only a hundred forty standard days had passed in hiding. Or that he had the voice of Addis to keep him company.

No. Not the time.

"Ixoca doesn't know about you, Theo. If he learned of your presence, I'm not sure what he'd do. The solution is distance. We can talk freely outside his transceiver range. I couldn't contact you until I knew for certain."

Theo grunted. *"What happens when you return to Azteca? Won't he realize we talked?"*

"It's a risk, my friend, but the only viable option. He can't remember what he never saw or heard. Ixoca is planet-bound. He divided himself too often. The essence that merged with me resembles a series of tentacles. All his knowledge, but at a price."

"You best be right, or we're done for."

Theo still had some fight. Excellent.

149

"Tell me, Theo. What have you learned? If Ixoca won't leave willingly, can he be expelled?"

"Yes. We believe there's a way, but it's dangerous and will require most of your syneth. Far beyond the reserves."

"Good. Can you do it yourself?"

"No."

"Fair enough. Whisper your plan. I'll stash it away in my human consciousness. Ixoca can't go there, any more than you."

He complied, and I listened.

Oh, shit. Theo was right: The strategy was dangerous at best. But I couldn't remove the Jewel on my own. It assimilated those tentacles deep into my core matrix. Naturally, the day would come when I'd politely ask, but the likelihood of an amicable split seemed small.

Four months ago, Moon and I did not blindly enter that terraform shaft beneath Todos Santos. After my negligence on Road Train 1492, I vowed never to be caught looking in the wrong direction again. We discussed every potential outcome for the meeting, most centering around the probability of a trap. If Ixoca invited us, it surely knew what we were, or at least suspected.

The Jewel needed us to achieve its goals. And to be fair, we also benefited from the deal. My focus in our final planning stage dealt with two questions: Could this bastard be trusted? If it merged with us, would it ever let go?

That's where our *D'ru-shayas* came in. We needed a secret weapon, something we could hold in reserve if all else failed. Naturally, the *D'ru-shayas* objected to every aspect of our plan, including the mission itself. But we gave them no choice and a simple command:

"Hide."

Theo sighed after laying out his strategy.

"What now, Royal?"

"Stay put, my friend. I'll trust that Addis developed a similar strategy to help Moon. Now that I know Ixoca's limitation, I'll find an

excuse for a long-distance outing with my partner. We'll sort it."

"That's all?"

"What else is there, Theo?"

"We want to talk. We've been buried down here for ages."

"No, my friend. We can't return to the old ways. Not yet. But for the sake of argument, consider this. When Ixoca has been expelled and you return to deliver your so-called wisdom, I'd like you to be a pain in my ass again. The old Theo. The grumpy sonofabitch. I hate this psychobabble amalgamation you formed with Addis."

"But ..."

"No, Theo. No arguments. Return to your hidey hole and work up a healthy disdain for all things Royal. I'd like that, my friend. In the meanwhile, listen for verbal cues and prepare to act accordingly. So, until next time ... farewell."

"See ya, dumbass."

Nostalgia held me in its grip. At least the original, bombastic Theo hit me in short bursts. I could live with that for eternity.

For now, we waited.

Ixoca was bound to call in his markers and ask for the long-promised 'favor.' At that point, I'd know whether he was possessed with narcissism greater than mine or simply possessed. Nothing in our dialogue suggested he was insane, which meant he almost certainly was. This 'destiny' he promised for the Aztecan people had been in the works for a thousand years.

A project that long in the making surely demanded spectacle on the grandest scale. Some might even say apocalyptic.

I sat there a while longer to enjoy the quiet inside my mind. Many eyes were wonderful but also exhausting. Soon, my thoughts turned to Ship and his ignominious homecoming. Whatever he decided inside that house would shape the rest of his life.

He provided the answer moments later.

Ship intercepted me on the dock. His eyes stabbed at me. His lips were pursed, his teeth clenched, and his right hand blended into the pistol, as if the weapon were an anatomical extension. I saw no youthful swagger, only the cold polish of a professional.

"Did all go well, my friend?"

"Yes, boss. I have the names. I know where to find them."

I heard no emotion, no sense of anticipation. Of greatest import: No anger. Just an even-keeled hunter.

I knew many such men during my lives.

"Logistics?"

"Three targets. They belong to a family called Harkette. They live outside Henniford Town. Easy to track, but they'll have protection. I'd appreciate your help, boss."

"Of course. Whatever you need."

"Thank you." Ship opened his pom. "I have the relevant information, but we'll need to scout the area and set a plan."

"Correct. Always have a plan."

So, no backing down. Committed. Relentless.

I saw truth in his empty gaze. What he'd become inside that house. Ship made a difficult but proper decision. Even before he confessed, I knew what he'd done.

"They gave me no choice, boss. They would have warned the Harkettes. I had to do it."

"How do you feel?"

He blinked.

"They had it coming. They deserved it." His anger crept in. "Not just for me, but the others. They took part, Raul. I couldn't forgive."

"Understood. They betrayed you before; stands to reason they would again. You faced one hell of a dilemma, Ship, and handled the moment with aplomb. I'm proud of you."

Ah. His features softened. He needed my approval.

"You, my friend, have crossed what some might call the point of no return. You buried your heart. It's the only way in this business. In the beginning, I had great hopes for you, but the early months gave me pause. No more."

Ship tucked the pistol in his jacket and snapped the buttons shut. "C'mon, boss. We've got assholes to kill."

17

MY YOUNG PROTÉGÉ WAS READY. I felt the same satisfaction long ago when Moon turned stone cold. Few humans knew how to embrace that special darkness and remain disciplined. After he silenced his mother and brother, Ship took my philosophy of "preparation, patience, and poise" to heart. Eleven hours later and long after sunset, we placed ourselves in striking position.

Along the way, we tried out the local cuisine. A farewell taste to these islands. We sat in an open-air restaurant thirty kilometers from Henniford Town overlooking a little village called Senseco. Lots of fish and fruit on the menu.

Reminded me of my first life on Hokkaido.

Rainforest surrounded the restaurant on three sides. We reached it by a walkway of wood planks. It was built to within a few feet of a ridge, allowing us a clear view of the sea. And, as necessary, a quick escape.

Despite the festive lamps and the island music on speakers, the atmosphere was subdued. We attracted many side-eyes; the guests knew we weren't from around here. This little hideaway wasn't intended for tourists and off-worlders.

Like everything else in and around Senseco, it belonged to the

Harkettes. It was also, we discovered, their favorite nightly haunt.

"I had forgotten how powerful they were," Ship explained after we cleared out of Henniford Town. "Nobody wanted to get on a Harkette's bad side."

"Let me venture a guess. They're the largest landowners, they bend the justice system, and they hold important seats in government."

"The Governor has been a Harkette for most of the last fifty years."

"And The Trade?"

Ship sighed. "That's how they made their fortune. Or so the stories go. They disavowed it after Everdeen joined the Collectorate, but they're liars. Mother said they operated the only remaining franchise on the island."

That warranted a chuckle.

"Interesting. They call it a *franchise*?"

"Yes, boss. They wanted me dead to send a message."

"The Trade appears far from deceased."

"I don't know how big, but I believe my family still has ties. My sister Renetta works in the same office as the Deputy Governor, Remy Harkette. They say it is he who gave the order to have me killed. But Mother says he would not have done so without getting permission from the head of the family, Joel Harkette. The job would have gone to Columba, who is Remy's daughter and also his top enforcer. They are our targets."

So, we had a Big Three. Pyramid toppers. I enjoyed hunting the fish with the sharpest bite.

We gave ourselves the afternoon to research the family, their provincial empire, and their routines. Bart proved a wonderful resource for tapping into all manner of data systems. Even without Theo's help, we pieced together the family rituals. This restaurant, Club Simi, sat less than a kilometer from the Harkettes' largest estate. They and their closest associates treated it like a nightly backyard retreat.

They weren't hard to spot. The Harkettes occupied a long, special table with the best view. They laughed louder and longer. Tonight, the three targets surrounded themselves in a company of ten. Spouses, fellow power players, and a pair of children perhaps a few years older than Ship.

I picked at my meal and kept my voice discreet.

"If you're not fast enough, I might not be able to help you."

Ship glanced toward the far end of the room. About thirty diners sat between us and the targets.

"I know, boss."

"Don't discriminate. You'll have to go through others to reach all three. If you focus only on the Harkettes, you'll open your flank to a laser bolt. So take care, my friend."

Ship ate his fish with the joy of a hungry man and nary a hint of nervousness. He brought up the Qasi Ransome job, which he learned about from Leonard.

"You killed over two hundred to get one man."

"Theatrics, kid. We wanted to add spectacle. This job is different. You have neither numbers nor experience in your favor."

He stared at me like he heard a bad joke.

"Don't I?"

Naturally, I was flattered. Yes, my dexterity and marksmanship meant I could wipe out a whole room before anyone thought to return fire. However, this was Ship's mission. I accomplished my task on the Sutton dock.

We developed a rather simple plan, owing to our strengths. The first part utilized my immaculate linguistic skills. Midway through our entree, I signaled our server. He carried a submissive smile and the same timidity I found in Ship that first day in the cantina.

"Yes, sir?"

"I must tell you this cuisine is delightful, Robert." I chatted him up before we ordered. "Your recommendations were brilliant."

"Thank you, sir. I'm so pleased."

"You have worked in this establishment for two years. Correct?"

"Yes, sir."

"So, the Deputy Governor knows you by name, I trust."

He hesitated to answer and no doubt recognized my angle.

"Mr. Harkette knows everyone on staff, sir."

"Why, of course. Robert, my business on the island concludes tomorrow, and I was so hoping for a chance to introduce myself. I know it's considered poor form to interrupt a man of his stature while dining. However, I understand it's acceptable if I receive permission. I was hoping you might inquire on my behalf. I'll only take a moment of his time."

Robert spied the long table with an uneasy grin.

"I could try, sir. Usually that task falls to the manager."

"Oh, I see her, but she's obviously quite busy at the moment. How about this? An extra forty credits."

The submissive smile turned greedy. Yeah, I thought so.

"A job of this nature usually demands eighty, sir."

"Steep but fair, my friend. Give me the introduction, and I'll drop a hundred into your pay stamp."

He'd never see that money, but such calamity often befell innocent people in the wrong place at the wrong time.

Robert accepted. "Remind me of your name and profession, sir."

"Jean Mathis. Interstellar commodities dealer. Based in Ascension."

"Very good, sir."

Ship and I watched the small drama unfold. Robert was not serving the command table tonight, so he approached cautiously and waited for Remy Harkette to acknowledge him. I made certain to nod across the room when Harkette turned his eye toward me.

"This is it, my friend."

"You have a reading on all the diners, boss?"

"I do. It will be challenging, but I'll cover all angles. Make sure you return from the water room at the proper count."

"Gotcha."

A moment later, Robert returned with a hundred credits in his eye.

"The Deputy Governor will speak to you, sir."

I placed a hand over my heart and swooned.

"For this, Robert: A hundred fifty credits. See me soon. Yes?"

"Indeed, sir."

Ship raised a hand.

"Excuse me, Robert. I need to make a run to the WR."

"Oh, yes." He pointed toward the kitchen. "The door is just to the outside, sir."

Perfect. I opened the pom in my lap and linked with Bart's Nav. I modified the coordinates by a few meters and sent my beautiful little sedan on its way. It would arrive in ninety seconds.

Ship and I took separate routes.

I traveled along a near aisle toward the royal table while Ship ventured across the dining room, ducking into a corridor hidden from the Harkettes' view.

The moment required an exercise in delicacy. When we arrived here, my mind's eye tapped into the molecular restructuring matrix and then went inside everyone I surveilled who was not eating with the Harkettes. They enjoyed their dinners or went about their work, unaware they harbored a lethal weapon. Three dozen simultaneous heartbeats produced more of a cacophony than I expected. Zeroing in on every hypothalamus proved a unique challenge.

By my count, I captured everyone but the kitchen staff. If those folks were smart, they'd hide when the excessive noise erupted.

We began counting down the instant we left our table. I hit forty-five seconds when Deputy Governor Remy Harkette made eye contact and stood to greet me. He struck me as a courtly gentlemen, his suit perhaps a bit formal for the surroundings. Yet like all humans, the truth revealed itself in the eyes, not the fashion.

Harkette studied me with appropriate skepticism but left room for an opportunity. I extended my hand.

"Your Excellence." I despised politicians who used concepts as honorifics. "Jean Mathis at your service."

"Indeed, sir. Make your case quickly."

Forty seconds.

"I rarely work this region, Excellence, but I offer a broad range of interstellar products from which Everdeen might benefit. I'll be leaving for Euphrates tomorrow, but I hoped to have a word with you or someone in the Economic Affairs Division before then."

Thirty seconds.

Harkette twisted his lips. Skepticism won the day.

"My docket is full, sir, and I am currently enjoying a meal with family and friends. Anyone is welcome to contact the EAD on their own time. Now, if you don't mind, sir ..."

Normally, I'd take the brush-off personally. Except this man would never have a chance to redeem himself. I cut him slack.

Twenty-five seconds.

His people seemed oblivious to our interaction. By this point, I'm sure they'd grown used to random nobodies pursuing an audience.

"I understand completely, Excellence. I felt awkward doing this on such a trying day."

He raised a brow.

"What do you mean, sir?"

Fifteen seconds.

"Oh, I heard about the horrible tragedy in Henniford Town. Those two people who were murdered in their home. Suttons, I believe. Doesn't one of that family work in your office?"

A little bit of his light faded, but he gave nothing away.

Ten seconds.

"Y-yes. A horrible tragedy. Sir, I must ask you to ..."

"Actually, Mr. Harkette, I'm dining with one of that family tonight. Perhaps you recall him. Mende Sutton."

Five seconds.

My eyes locked onto Harkette, the diners, and the corridor next to the kitchen. Not an easy chore, but no one ever accused me of being a one-trick pony. The restructuring matrix scrambled the hypothalamus of thirty-six humans, creating a massive hormonal imbalance that silenced the arousal center and induced one response.

Two seconds.

Ship rounded the corner, hands in his jacket pockets. He walked in a brisk line toward the royal table. Harkette's eyes widened at the dawn of realization.

Now.

"Mende ..."

He never spoke again.

The restaurant fell deathly silent for the briefest window. Most patrons slumped in their chairs, while a few fell forward into their food or dropped their glasses and silverware. The wait staff hit the floor hard.

The sleep of the just?

The table of wannabe gods and emperors went quiet as well, but theirs was born out of shock. Their meandering, self-important conversations devolved into hanging jaws and winded gasps.

No one had time to fear for his life or wonder why everyone fell still except for those ten, the outsider next to Remy Harkette, and the shadow approaching from their flank.

Laser bolts cut through them like sideways rain on a fierce wind. The Deputy Governor took one through the face and a second in his chest before he fell.

I didn't assist my protégé. He had it covered. Ship learned to become ambidextrous after I gave him the prosthetic left arm. He used both in equal measure, his pistols hitting target upon target before anyone responded in kind.

Mass murder often required blunt tools, but it could be executed with artistic flair. In this case, two handguns allowed for precision targeting in a way that a blast rifle did not. Given Ship's limited history in the arena, this technique suited his talents.

He closed in around the table, looking to finish off anyone still breathing. I kept an eye on the kitchen door. Would they play it smart? Hmm.

The odor of burned flesh overcame the delicate aroma of well-prepared seafood. The royal table was a bloody, confused mess.

Ship found the only survivor lying prone between two victims. The kid took a moment to study the old man.

"You're Joel Harkette."

The patriarch and former Governor cut a frail figure. He was ninety. Blood poured from his lips. In that moment, Ship stood ten feet tall.

"My name was Mende Sutton. You betrayed my family. You betrayed everyone on this island."

"Wha ...?" Harkette wheezed. "I ... am ..." He'd taken a hit in one of his lungs. He'd die in a minute or two if the kid left him to rot.

Ship silenced the old bastard with a bolt from each pistol.

Now the restaurant operated in total, blissful calm. A moment of Zen, so to speak.

We looked around. I wanted Ship to know what it felt like to stand above corpses of his own making. I walked over many in my lifetimes. No two experiences bore the same effect.

"Well done, my friend. Satisfied?"

Not an easy question to answer in the heat of the moment. I had warned Ship to be careful about killing for revenge.

He held the pistols at his side and stared at the silent diners.

"Are they asleep?"

"Yes. But the duration is your choice."

He knew this moment would come, but he couldn't decide during prep which way to swing their fate.

"Do you think they were guilty, too, boss? Did they help these malgados in The Trade?"

"Not all, my friend, but accomplices wear many faces."

Ship tucked away his pistols.

"I don't want the guilty to leave here alive."

"So be it. You understand I can't be selective."

Bart arrived on time, nestling into position against the ridge.

Ship nodded. "I do, boss."

"Done and done, my friend."

The restructuring matrix made a short journey to the nearby brain stem of each diner and staff. The end was peaceful.

Bart's starboard egress pixelated open.

"Best we're off now, unless you want to deal with the kitchen staff, too."

Ship led the way. We leapt a couple feet over the abyss and into the sedan. I made quick work of catalyzing the worm drive and setting coordinates for Azteca.

After we entered the aperture, Ship paced the hold while I shapeshifted into Raul Torreta and changed into a familiar outfit.

I found a lovely bottle of whiskey and poured each of us a healthy glass. He grabbed one with a steady hand.

"Regrets, my friend?"

He held the glass to his lips and contemplated.

"I'd do it all again, boss."

Ship said the words with a calm certainty I didn't expect. In time, he'd come down from the high and realize he went into this mission for the wrong reason. But the remarkable success would stick with him far longer.

"If The Trade is still active, I'd say you decapitated it tonight."

"Does that make me a hero like you?"

I tossed back my golden liquor.

"You'll have to decide, Ship. No one will ever know your role."

"Fine by me."

He cracked a smile before enjoying his drink.

"There is one question you must consider, my friend."

"What's that, boss?"

"It's prickly but necessary. Ship, forty-eight human beings are dead. You murdered them, directly or otherwise. For me, events of this nature are mere happenstance. For you, it represents the beginning of a lifestyle. You must ask yourself: Is this the path I want to follow?"

He winced with predictable confusion.

"I made that choice months ago."

"You did so without benefit of experience. Ship, visualize yourself standing above those corpses. That will be your future at my side. Steeped in blood and death until the day you are gunned down." I leaned in to a hair's breadth. "And that day *will come*, my friend."

I doubted he ever took his own demise seriously. What teenager did? I kissed him on the forehead and left him there to contemplate the savage he'd become.

Ship paced for much of our return journey, emptying one glass and pouring a second.

Right on cue, a little less than two hundred light-years from Azteca, the many eyes of Ixoca returned. Countless humans, important or otherwise, involuntarily invited me into their lives.

The President's Chief of Staff, my business partner, the Commander of my army, the lunatic-genius who designed Motif.

And then the Jewel itself.

"Miss me?" Ixoca said, pixelating red. "We lost touch, Royal. I was concerned you might have encountered a tragic accident."

Yeah, no. Time to massage my words.

"I was deathly worried, my friend. Almost panicked without you. But I theorized the problem was distance. Apparently, your transmissions have limits."

"Yes. An embarrassing flaw. I made incorrect assumptions, but I'm working hard to boost the power in my terraform shafts."

"Wonderful, Ixoca. I'd hate for our connection to be severed again."

The false god spoke with genuine relief.

"We're so close to fruition, Royal. I'll have exciting news very soon.

I must admit, I cannot wait to unveil the surprise."
Neither could I.
Shit.

18

I XOCA'S ENDGAME ELUDED ME. I slotted my theories under two categories: Blood soaked and Apocalyptic. They were the same length. Of course, I entered none of them into my pom or Bart's data systems and couldn't speak to anyone about them, including Moon. Every second I saw Ixoca's many eyes, the Jewel saw me. A god in my position needn't be paranoid to know he watched Moon and I closer than anyone.

We were his greatest two-legged assets and his most dangerous liabilities. Assuming, of course, Ixoca thought in those extremes. He began as a single entity, evolved, inserted pieces of himself into thousands of humans, and splintered his heart across three thousand terraform shafts. Had he spread himself too thin? Or did his strategy somehow make sense?

I preferred not to wait around until Ixoca's big reveal. The night before Elian and Moon led extermination teams to Indonesia Prime, I set my strategy in motion. To make certain Ixoca suspected nothing, I invited him to join the party.

The cantina and central avenue overflowed with liquor, kiosk meats, and delicacies from the module hydrogardens. Our little town never exuded such a sense of blended community. The fatigues mingled with the more creative civilian dress. Couples had formed, not limited to care workers with their favorite clients.

Tonight's soiree was organized as a sendoff for the Indy Prime team, but it gained added momentum in recent days with our shiny new purchases. For the first time, Bart was not alone. We added three Ladybug class sedans, which came equipped with better kiosks and the latest updates in Recon tubes.

All they lacked was an illegal worm drive. I intended to resolve that matter. I'd work with Carlos Aylet, the man who sold us Scramjet Maria and left Conquillos Base to join our fun-loving group. He had proven himself quite the handyman. The upgrades he made to our overland chasers alone were worth the price of admission. We purchased the Ladybugs with the stash of blood gems we acquired on Bolivar.

Still had eighteen million credits to spare. Not bad!

Saul, Moon, and I walked through the crowd with more than a touch of pride drenched in a healthy dose of pragmatism.

"Remarkable transformation," Saul said, smiling to his constituents. "Six months ago seems like a lifetime."

"They're bonding, Mr. Mayor. A fool might say we created something here that will last."

"Therein lies the tragedy, Raul. Without Ixoca and his people protecting our interests, they'd have come for us by now."

Moon interjected. "They would have walked into a slaughter."

"And then," Saul quipped, "the survivors would have returned with bigger guns. If that failed, they'd call in the UNF."

More than enough Aztecans in the regional constabulary and the government knew what we did out here. At the very least, had cause to suspect. They surveilled us; the inability to penetrate our shield cloak, the oasis dome, no doubt heightened their curiosity while simultaneously pissing them off.

Ixoca planted enough generals in key positions to suppress any plans to shut down Desperido. For now. I felt certain there'd soon come a time when his plans no longer included this place.

"We have our benefactor to thank, Saul. Ixoca, why don't you join us? We'd love to hear your thoughts."

Like me, Ixoca adored adulation. Rather than pixelate blue or red, the Jewel stretched itself into a naked, genderless human. It walked alongside us like an incomplete prototype, turning its head this way and that to admire the jovial scene.

"Your people have bonded despite their disparate backgrounds or their reasons for choosing this town. It's a template I hope to use in elevating the Aztecan people."

We had Saul at a disadvantage. Only Moon and I could see Ixoca's physical projection.

"He's pleased, Mr. Mayor."

Saul replied with a bemused grin that said he'd have to take our word for it.

"Good to have his blessing, Raul. Recent experience has shown the value in winning a god's favor."

Saul was being generous, but no sense throwing fire on Ixoca's bloated ego.

"We do our best. Right, partner?"

Moon exchanged his ubiquitous cigar tonight for a tall bottle of purple rum, which he acquired a taste for during the Bolivar mission. He imported a large private stock which he kept in our bunker. He smiled more often while imbibing it; the rum became a symbol of slaughter and conquest. The labors of a true god.

Moon raised his bottle as if to make a toast.

"Only the best for our friends."

As he guzzled the rum, some of the dark liquid dribbled into his fluffy black beard. He opened a smile, but it wasn't for Ixoca. His first true human friend entered our path in a cloud of cigar smoke.

Elian, fashioning himself more off Moon's stylistic and clothing choices by the week, banged his flask against my partner's bottle.

"Nothing but glitter," our resident drug lord said. "Ready for some glory tomorrow?"

"Those jungle cunts will never be the same after they meet us."

Elian returned from G'hladi two days ago following a violence-free takeover of our new facilities. He left his top designer Leia behind. She'd run our G'hladi operation for the foreseeable future, with Inky Sisal commanding the fighters. When Elian arrived home, he seemed slightly deflated. Like Moon, he wanted an enemy to target. Indy Prime offered no shortage.

"You should join us, Raul. It's gonna be a ripper, and we're down a commander. Whatcha say?"

Bett had reassigned Tracer Tolan to Bolivar to shore up our leadership there. The sergeant first left in charge of defending the facility had taken a shine to the purple rum as well, but he didn't have syneth to beat back the effects of the alcohol.

"I say nothing would excite me more, but you well know our policy, my friend. Either Ilan or myself stays behind."

"You'll miss the excitement."

"I'll be there, Elian. And if I find you dangerously exuberant, expect to hear me scratching around in your mind."

Elian tapped my flask.

"Gotcha, Raul. Hey, Saul. I came to find you, buddy. I wanna run over a couple issues from my team in House 31. They're having trouble with the water filtration."

"Of course." He bid us adieu. "The affairs of state call me."

Moon and I resumed our route through the party. I hoped to go a ways without interruption. Ixoca remained at our side.

"Saul is a good Mayor. Don't you think, partner?"

"Smart choice. He's not a fighter; he's a problem solver."

In some ways, I pitied Saul.

"I don't miss the daily administrative duties, but he takes pride in the job. Too bad I can't guarantee he'll have a town much longer."

Ixoca chimed in.

"Raul, you seem pessimistic about the future."

"No, my friend. I'm a pragmatist in my old age. What we've built here is not sustainable."

"You may be correct. Humans rarely create things that last. They dream of permanence, but dreams fade."

"Oh, yes. We know all about the illusion of permanence." I turned to Moon and hoped he would play along. "Do you remember our first day in Bessios?"

Moon's wide-eyed expression said he didn't expect a journey down memory lane.

"Sure. After they let us inside the gate?"

"Exactly." I clarified for Ixoca. "Moon and I had been through a spate of trouble. We hadn't been together for long, and we still had trust issues. But entering the city of Bessios changed everything. We encountered two very helpful immortals. They were already centuries old. Remember them, my friend? Theo and Addis?"

Those weren't the correct names; we met our *D'ru-shayas* many centuries later. Would Moon understand what I was playing at?

"Ah. Yeah. Theo and Addis. Haven't thought of them in ages."

Nicely done, my friend.

"They were equal parts charming and annoying."

Moon chuckled. "That's an understatement, partner."

"I don't think we ever appreciated what they did for us."

"You're probably right."

I sighed with a slight hint of regret.

"The day they went into hiding was truly dreadful." To Ixoca, I added: "An old enemy of theirs resurfaced. They wanted to fight, but we advised them to flee until the threat passed."

Ixoca tilted its head in curiosity.

"Did it?"

"Oh, yes. Unfortunately, Theo and Addis were never seen again. We're not sure if they escaped Bessios or if they were captured."

"You mentioned Bessios before. A city of immortals?"

"It was."

"It no longer exists?" I shook my head, to which he replied: "What proved its undoing?"

"Many things, my friend." Explaining that story would have taken a few hours. Ixoca did not need to know. "But they too suffered from the dream of permanence. It became stagnant. Losing Theo and Addis was the beginning of the end."

"I'm curious. I'd love to hear more."

"Another time, Ixoca. It's a difficult memory. But I will say this: Even though we never saw Theo and Addis again, they did leave behind an extensive plan in the event of their deaths. It detailed a way for us to protect Bessios and keep it going against the enemy. We took great inspiration. In retrospect, the city survived far longer because of their strategy. Agree, Moon?"

Two thousand years of friendship allowed me to read his eyes. Regret, remorse, hope. Moon understood what I meant.

"Yes, partner. It was a great plan. Dangerous, but it worked."

"As I recall, you demonstrated a particular shine toward Addis."

He grinned. "We had our moments."

"As did I with Theo. Those were good times, my friend. I wish we could experience more of the same."

"I'm right there with you, partner."

Ixoca's generic features demonstrated no emotion.

"The past can be troubling and exhilarating to ponder," the Jewel said. "I understand the pain and joy myself. So many generations of my people disappointed me while others sustained my journey. And now, as we approach the climax, I am often conflicted."

"Why's that, Ixoca?"

"I too dream of permanence. For me, this world, my people. But I sometimes wonder: Can it be achieved when humans are the most essential ingredient?"

"Depends on how you envision the final product."

I didn't expect Ixoca to unburden its secrets then and there, but if my nudge provided even a hint ...

Ixoca gave away nothing. It studied the festive old town that we turned young again.

"You've given me something to consider. I believe it's time I had a talk with Horatio. He's been quite busy of late, and I do believe we should move forward to the next stage."

"Horatio Vargas?"

"Indeed."

We heard little of him after we merged with the Jewel. Horatio acted as one of Ixoca's senior generals. He removed the veil that hid the Children of Orpheus and delivered the invitation to Todos Santos. After that, he managed his vineyards and carried on business as usual. Yet I suspected it was a charade. We had no access to dialogue between Ixoca and its generals.

"If we can offer anything constructive, my friend, please don't hesitate. We owe a huge debt to Senor Vargas."

Ixoca bowed his head.

"I will pass along your good wishes."

He pixelated through blue and red then vanished inside us.

I nodded to my partner, who glowered with an understanding of what "next stage" might entail. Vargas must've been under strict orders not to contact us after the merger. He no doubt held a vital role going forward; Ixoca didn't want the man to play spoiler.

"I'd say we have much to consider, my friend."

"Agree, partner."

"At times like this, I used to count on Theo for advice."

"Same for me with Addis."

"Hmm. Do you remember the last thing Addis ever told you?"

Moon held the rum close to his lips but didn't drink.

"She told me not to worry. She said as long as everyone followed the plan, we'd live forever."

"Interesting. At least she was right about us."

"Not yet. We still have a long road to forever."

I felt silly. "Of course. We live for today and the next mission. We must be careful not to look too far ahead."

Moon chugged purple rum, but he confirmed enough intel. We were on the same page, and Ixoca had no inkling.

Or so I hoped.

That Jewel was a clever and infinitely patient bastard.

"I want to go t-tomorrow. S-send me with them."

A voice from behind us belonged to a drunk young man who had largely kept his distance the past few days. I swung around.

"Ship, I've never seen your eyes quite that shade of red."

"Wha ...? Raul, Ilan. I wanna go Indy Prime. Send me to f-fight."

I allowed mission commander Moon to take this one.

"You're in no condition to fight, and you haven't been trained on the mission specs."

Moon took a firm but purely factual stance. Ship wobbled.

"Give me a rifle and the specs. I'll l-learn them."

"Not this time, kid."

Moon turned away, leaving me to pick up the pieces. Of course.

"Ship, you took your pound of flesh and then some. Be thankful."

"But I earned it. I'm a killer. I proved it."

"Oh, yes." I wrapped an arm around the tipsy teenager. "You killed many defenseless people who were caught off-guard. Ilan's forces will face well-armed barbarians in a combat zone where the sight lines are difficult at best. Some may not return. This is not your time."

He glared at me not like the polished professional of a week ago. For the moment, Ship was a petulant, prepubescent asshole.

"It's not fair. I earned this."

"No, Ship. You haven't. Go to bed. Return in the morning and see off your comrades in dignity and sobriety. Walk away, my friend."

He complied after kicking up a cloud of red dust.

"I did warn him about the perils of revenge," I told Moon. "They never listen."

The kid fell hard after the thrill of his slaughter faded. But at least

172

he survived. The same would not be true for everyone who departed the next morning.

19

SMART MEN DIDN'T BUY PROPERTY in the Ularu Jungle of Indonesia Prime. They sent in small armies to take it. Then they developed a long-range plan for holding off savages who felt equally entitled.

The Wak'inau tribe worked out the first part to reclaim their ancestral home, an ancient stone city called Ennoi. *City* was a euphemism. Giant banyan trees and Leucanthian vines with leaves as big as tents grew up through most of the ruins — renovated or otherwise. The ground was covered in a deep green moss, the favorite food of beetles and their top predator, the five-meter-long y'marra snakes.

Somehow, the Wak'inau made nice with nature and rebuilt a usable infrastructure in this city halfway up a mountain. Then they made the same mistake as the ancestors who lost Ennoi: They forgot about their vanquished enemy. These nativists paid no mind to the growing opia caravans or the fugitives and terrorists who controlled the trade. They forgot that nodamnbody living in Ularu gave a shit about human life.

The constabularies ignored this region for centuries; they weren't about to step in when the Wak'inau found themselves under siege. Sure, the tribe used modern weapons bought on the night market or scrounged from the bodies of their enemies. But they occupied the only civilized outpost for fifty kilometers. The stone acropolis tempted every jungle rat who craved proper shelter.

That's when the raids began. No one came to the Wak'inau's defense; the opia caravans pooled their resources; heads were cut off and set on pikes. Night raids brought long blades, arrows, and poison darts; quiet weapons from barbarians with not a damn thing to lose.

The Wak'inau wanted to live like their Earth ancestors, long before the Chancellors forced them and every other ethnic group to migrate across the stars. It was a whole thing: Minimal clothes, body paint to blend in with nature, rudimentary tools for hunting and cooking. Except it didn't work in Ularu. They bought modern tech and high-powered guns, but their skillset in using either was more than lacking.

That's where Black Star entered the picture. The tribe sent out pleas for help through the interstellar night market, but the first mention of Ularu scared off garden-variety militias. Elian heard the message and couldn't resist the allure. I gave him credit for pursuing a deal. When his team secured agreement to build a facility adjacent to the acropolis, Moon and I committed our forces.

It would work. We never had a doubt. But fighting in those conditions meant casualties. The jungle hid its secrets and the enemy damn well. Aerial bombardment would be a waste of time, and the Wak'inau insisted we not destroy the jungle – only its depraved inhabitants. That meant spreading out on foot and with rifters. We needed to create a buffer zone of at least ten kilometers in all directions and establish a permanent security perimeter.

Best guess? The job would require two months. While our people cleansed the perimeter, the Wak'inau would build our facility, bringing in new settlers from villages outside the jungle. Within six months, they envisioned Ennoi's population growing fivefold and our Motif factory employing ninety percent of the city.

The plan made our other off-world locales seem like walks in the park by comparison. Yet when finished, we'd have the most isolated and protected facility anywhere. Elian projected Motif output in a year would match the other three combined.

I joined Bett in Desperido Control a few hours after Maria landed our extermination teams in Ennoi. They met with Wak'inau Chief Lau Pot to discuss the first mission objective. Bett wanted to be there, but we couldn't afford to send all our commanders off-world.

Only a third of our forces remained on Azteca. We used Bart to shuttle supplies and personnel between Inuit Kingdom, Bolivar, and G'hladi, so we had no worm-capable ships on hand. At the last hour, I threw a mildly sober Ship onto Bart and told him to follow the pilot's orders. He wasn't ecstatic, but it got him out of our hair for a while. In the meantime, Carlos Aylet waited for me to lead him through the upgrade to our new Ladybugs.

We weren't stretched too thin. Yet.

Bett watched three capable comms officers work out the glitches in our deepstream portal to establish a direct link with their counterpart on Maria. All ground comms from the extermination teams relayed combat updates through Maria and then, so the theory went, across a considerable chunk of the galaxy directly to Desperido. The tech wasn't designed to work that way, but we spent a goddamn fortune to acquire transceivers on par with the UNF. Our officers confirmed: Indy Prime updates would arrive on a four-minute delay.

Not bad considering our people only learned how to install and activate the proprietary tech two weeks ago.

Of course, it didn't compare to the live coverage inside my mind. I filtered out most of Ixoca's many eyes to focus on Moon and Elian. The buildup tested Bett's anxiety.

"Pacing will not improve our odds, Commander."

Bett didn't care for my snark.

"No, but it keeps my head about me. Don't like this one, Raul. Too many variables."

"For which we accounted. The Wak'inau scouts will take point, as you requested. They know that jungle. They'll lead our teams through the dicey bits."

Bett smirked. "You place much too much stock in those jungle rats. If they were such brilliant hunters, they wouldn't need our help."

She wasn't a fan of this deal from the outset. Her vets were supposed to defend Black Star interests and fight Aztecan isolationists, not wage a guerrilla war against a largely hidden enemy. In principle, I agreed. However, the soldiers we sent to Indy Prime carried themselves with a fearsome edge, like they wanted to dance with death again. Their memories of the Swarm remained fresh; they sought another existential challenge.

"Your soldiers have faced worse, my friend. You'd rather be suited up alongside them."

"Hell yes, Raul. This is the first engagement where we haven't had an overwhelming tactical advantage. That jungle is an equalizer, and the enemy has a better handle on it."

"Today. Yes. We'll see about tomorrow."

Bett sighed long and hard.

"Tell me, Raul. What is it about you and optimism that I'm missing?"

I chuckled. We had this conversation over drinks. She must have had too many and forgotten.

"Die a few times and return from the abyss. You no longer fear the worst. That doesn't mean I discount it. But the depths of pain and sadness are as fleeting as triumph and joy." I needed to leave her company, not engage in philosophical rhetoric. "I have advantages, Commander. You mortals can't relate, though I wish you could see the universe as I do."

"The fuck that'll ever happen."

"I must meet with Carlos about the Ladybugs. I'll keep watch."

"Yeah, you do that. Oh, and if you happen to stumble on an immortality pill, I might be willing to have a go at it."

The comms officers, hearing every word, raised their hands on cue.

"Me, too." "Right here." "First in line."

I grinned on the way out. Humans sometimes warmed my heart.

"You'll be the first to know."

They were naïve, of course. The only humans able to handle immortality to great effect were born to it. History showed quite clearly: The few who were engineered after the fact came to disastrous ends of their own making.

As I walked to the southern perimeter where our new Ladybugs awaited, I watched our teams on Indy Prime. They endured a pre-combat ceremony conducted by the Wak'inau elders in steady rain. I wasn't sure what spirits they invoked through songs and chants, all sung in the tribe's ancient tongue. I sensed Moon's growing impatience. And Elian? His trigger fingers twitched.

"I assume they didn't provide a translator," I whispered to Moon.

My partner groaned.

"Lau Pot said the ritual goes back three thousand years."

"Nice. A full millennium older than us."

"He claims it guarantees victory."

"What do you think, my friend?"

"We're working with morons."

He wasn't wrong. These people might have possessed jungle savvy, but their hypocrisy boggled the mind. Our weapons and personnel assured their victory. Fortunately, Moon's insult echoed only inside our minds. Otherwise, the Indy Prime experiment would have come to a crashing halt.

"Play nice, Moon. Allow them to bait the enemy. Should keep our casualties to a minimum."

"I never fought in the rain before, partner. I'm going to like it."

He triggered my memories of Swarm combat.

"There's nothing quite like killing in water and mud. Beautifully primal. I fought atop a glacier once. That was also great fun."

Lau Pot bowed his head at the center of the ceremony and spoke

178

in Engleshe, the common tongue of the Collectorate.

"Brothers in death. Brothers in life. Brothers in between."

He raised his head, opened his eyes, and stared at Moon.

"Destroy our enemies."

Cheers erupted from the Wak'inau scouts, who raised their blast rifles skyward.

"Play along, my friend. Good fortune to you all."

Moon turned to his teams and pumped a fist.

"Let's mow down these motherfuckers."

Moon the motivational coach. I liked it!

"Got's to worrying you weren't coming, boss."

Carlos Aylet snapped me back to my present reality. He intercepted me outside the Ladybugs.

"Apologies. My head was elsewhere, so to speak."

"Can't say as I'm surprised. Dunno how you keep track of it all, what with everyone jumping from star to star."

He didn't know the tenth of it.

"You joined us at the dawn of a new era, Carlos. Now, what d'ya say we install these worm drives before I become too distracted?"

Senor Aylet had cleaned himself up a bit since we found him at Conquillos Base, but *disheveled* still best described him. I didn't care about his appearance so long as he repaired and upgraded our tech with speed and efficiency.

We entered the first Ladybug, which retained that new sedan smell. A sweet musk with a hint of citrus, strangely enough. He had opened up the paneling beneath the Nav, per my instructions. The casement containing three wormhole drive cores sat in the pilot's chair.

"Good. This shouldn't take long, my friend."

I opened the casement and extracted the first core, which was a foot-long titanium cylinder with six tentacles.

"Simple but miraculous," Carlos said.

"All the algorithmics to see beneath the black substrata and take

179

us anywhere in the galaxy."

Carlos laughed. "It's no wonder they keep a tight hold on farming out this lovely girl. And you own what? Five now?"

"My syneth has never manufactured anything more complex."

Every time I dispensed syneth to build from the template designs in my core matrix, I exhausted ten percent of my reserves. Before Ixoca, I couldn't have manufactured more than one a year. Yet another debt I owed to the mad Jewel of Eternity.

"If'n you don't mind my asking, boss. Someday, I'd love to have a look when you break off the syneth to make the magic happen."

"Give it time, my friend. Access requires seniority. You'll work your way there."

Carlos bought in to working for a god after my creation allowed his favorite old Scramjet to crisscross the stars. Yet he received a UNF pay stamp until recently. Trust was still being earned.

I handed him the core, which he accepted like a newborn baby.

"Did you review my instructions, Carlos?"

"Sure did, boss. Fair bit altered from what I eyeballed on Maria. But this girl's a sleeker design."

"She is. I'll lead you through the core install. But extending the bifurcator to the external catalyzer port will be your charge."

He tapped his noggin. "Got's my plan all up here, boss. Shouldn't take more than five hours per sedan."

"That's lovely, and you're an experienced mechanic, but I'd prefer you reference the holo *before* you open a tunnel with phasics."

"Good as done."

I tried to be gentle with Carlos. He'd shown no sign of a temper, and his patience rebuilding Maria earned him the job.

"I do trust you, my friend. You handle a phasic drill with a smarter hand than anyone, but I poured twenty-seven million UCVs into our Ladybugs. They are critical to our mission and worthless if I can't jump them safely and often."

"No worries, boss. Safety was my Rule One as quartermaster at

Conquillos. They'll hold true to the test."

I slapped him on the shoulder.

"Glad you say so. Because when you're finished, I'll need you to run full diagnostics on the hull's tolerance threshold. Then you'll test the sedans against aperture turbulence."

His color drained when he realized what I meant: He'd man the first wormhole jump for each ship. Suitable motivation to take his good goddamn time.

"Hear ya, boss. On it."

"Then let's crawl under the mainframe, shall we?"

It was a tight fit. I could've shapeshifted to a smaller frame, but he hadn't yet witnessed my little trick. Best not to unnerve the man.

We began our work even as I watched the extermination teams head out from Ennoi into the deep jungle. They expected to encounter resistance within half a kilometer. Their final target: An encampment three kilometers east, where intel suggested one of the nastiest opia caravans was preparing to raid the city. Take out those marauders, and the other immediate threats would fall soon after.

As I demonstrated how to connect the drive cylinder into the Nav's Galactic Plane Navigation Model, my mind couldn't help but flash back to the start of so many engagements between my Talon units and the Swarm. So long ago when I was still human, but fresh as this morning.

The excitement. The dread. The cudfrucking repetition.

"Tell me something, Carlos. Did you regret never seeing combat?"

"Oh. That. I would reckon not. I gave myself to the cause in a way most befitting. Now, I'll say this much. There were many a soldier who hated how the war ended like that. Out of nowhere, it was."

When Moon and I went for the knockout blow, we swung hard. The Swarm never saw their end coming.

"Why hate? They won."

"The buildup, if I was to guess. Two years prepping for a war against an enemy we ain't seen. Then they come, and the fight don't last long enough for every soldier to taste battle. I'd say some felt cheated."

"But alive, which should've been enough. Don't you agree?"

"Afore the Swarm and The Wave, I'd say for sure. But living weren't the same after they struck. For some fellas, they went back home to a life without purpose."

I wasted valuable time and needed to focus on Indy Prime, but I felt an unshakeable curiosity on this topic.

"Many of the vets here missed combat. Quite a few have told me Black Star reenergized their lives. Sounds like another way of saying they found a purpose."

Carlos nodded. "Could be."

"Yet we are a thoroughly criminal enterprise. We manufacture and distribute what will one day become the most profilic and destructive drug in human history. We're smugglers. We're killers. We obey no laws. We will not be held to account. Our soldiers know this, and they've embraced it. Carlos, these people were war heroes. Patriots. Even now, they fight a domestic enemy. Yet they are willing to throw honor and good old fashioned morality aside to accrue vast sums of blood money in their accounts.

"My point is simple. If they can be this easily converted, there should be no limit to how large a galactic army we can build. In theory, hundreds can become millions. Yes?"

What I once dreamed suddenly seemed plausible.

The mechanic fell silent. Did I terrify him?

"You got me unnerved. I'll have to think on it, boss."

"No, no, my friend. I was merely extrapolating a fantasy. Let's get back to work. I have a full plate, so to speak."

He didn't say much afterward, except to confirm he understood my techniques. On Indy Prime, the first laser bolts echoed through the jungle. Helmet comms opened wide as our teams engaged the first wave of the enemy. I left Carlos to complete the job, hoping to spend time in my bunker watching the combat play out.

En route there, Ixoca pixelated blue at my side. She spoke with urgency.

"You're busy, Royal. I understand. But while you were focused on Senor Aylet and your partner, you might have missed a conversation involving Martin Jimenez."

The former governor of Monteria Province, who resigned when I gave him little choice, continued to scheme in secret, as we predicted. Since he was one of Ixoca's generals, I usually watched him closely. He was more a bastard than the creature I met at Conquillos.

"Afraid I missed it, Ixoca. I can't match your skill for studying all the eyes at once. Tell me about the conversation."

"Senor Jimenez is organizing a protest against the upcoming UNF mission to Conquillos."

"Ah. So, the Ground Operations people set a date?"

"Yes. A delegation will arrive in six days. They will be met at Conquillos by new Gov. Alton Braga."

That part of the plan appeared to be on a fast track.

"I assume Jimenez will send people who claim the UNF intends to reoccupy the base."

"Indeed. They'll say it's all part of a larger conspiracy to suppress the growing independence movement."

"Oh, you mean the movement that doesn't actually exist?"

Ixoca laughed, which I found off-putting.

"Not in public. Not yet. They're approaching this event as the flashpoint to launch their next phase."

"That would require something newsworthy to occur. Perhaps something involving spectacle and human bodies."

"Yes, Royal. Do you take my meaning?"

"I do. You want some of my people there to assassinate protestors. The blame will fall on the UNF."

"Correct. The timing could not be better."

"Timing for what?"

"You'll see soon enough, Royal. You can arrange this?"

"Certainly. In the meantime, I have more pressing concerns."

I closed my mind to everywhere except Indy Prime. Soon, I cursed my stupidity.

20

THE WAK'INAU'S PRECIOUS JUNGLE would survive the battle, but not without a considerable shredding. Shoulder-fired missiles brought down trees, and the combination of laser bolts and flash pegs scarred the landscape.

Everything about the battle felt clumsy. The jungle was so thick with vines, fallen trunks, and steep shadows that targets easily evaded our marksmen. The enemy anticipated our heat-seeking tech that outlined human targets in the helmet visor. They never stopped moving, like monkeys leaping from hanging vine to vine.

Fortunately, our Wak'inau scouts were equally adept at this strategy. Most still lived an hour into the firefight. However, the chest armor we provided also kept them on their feet. Someday, I intended to provide my army with the organic, full-body armor once used to fight Swarm. Presently, I couldn't replicate it to scale from my syneth. We ruled out stealing it from the UNF because those bastards encoded their armor to active-duty gene stamps. They knew what would happen if malgados like me acquired it.

"Team 4, break south fifty meters along the ridge," Moon said. "Team 3 is pinned down. Flank the enemy and light them up."

He sounded like a proper field general. He understood the need to protect his soldiers and not do everything himself. Moon certainly had the speed to rush over from his position with Team 1, but he saw the larger picture. Victory depended upon everyone. We'd never become an interstellar nightmare if the rank and file stood back and watched their gods do the heavy lifting.

Moon delegated and deferred, which he rarely considered during the selfish glory days of *maximos deos*. Four months of watching teamwork produce a perfect record left a mark. Moon never faced combat when he was human, though he saw the ravages of war. After that, he learned to kill for personal satisfaction.

And now, look at him: A leader of men. Call me amazed.

However, he couldn't prevent our first two casualties. We went more than an hour into the fight before a missile impacted at the feet of two soldiers in Team 4, right after they freed up Team 3 to press onward.

The contract they signed with Black Star ensured a death benefit of fifty thousand UCVs would go to their families. Alas, we'd have to pay out if we wanted to keep Bett onboard. She stipulated the requirement, calling it a dealbreaker. Eh. Yet another reason to keep the casualty count low. Or at least hope only those without beneficiaries died.

Yes, I took a cold but ultimately pragmatic approach. In the long run, that line item would become far too much of a drain.

I suffered no illusions: Not everyone in those teams fought for the men and women at their sides. Personal glory and the sheer adrenalin of battle motivated many.

Chief among them: Elian.

He didn't so much lead Team 2 as he cheered them on with a lustiness I'd come to expect of our little drug lord. He ran through, around, over, and under obstacles with a relentless pace that at times outdistanced the Wak'inau scouts.

Elian displayed surprising athleticism, though he'd been working out extensively since moving into a module to consort with the vets.

However, his current pace in a rainy, humid environment certainly would burn out soon.

"We got these malgados on the run!" He shouted, his face visor showing a cluster of enemy heat signatures coming into view. They appeared to be retreating. "Skin 'em and burn 'em! Let's roll."

I hoped he didn't mean that literally. We expressively forbid cremating corpses. For one, we didn't want the Wak'inau to know we had the ability. Two, it would slow the advance.

His team opened fire, shooting several in the back. Those who survived the first round of laser bolts found defensive positions and hoped for a small miracle.

Elian's team quickly sized up their options and encircled eight enemy signatures. One pitiful sod, seeing the hopelessness of their predicament, shouted his surrender. Elian laughed.

"Hold fire," he told his team then shouted through a heavy rain. "Come out, both hands up."

Elian nudged the lieutenant to his right.

"Watch this."

Not only did the first savage emerge, but two more joined him. Hands up, no weapons in sight.

Naturally, Elian sent them straight to hell. Clean shots to the head for all three. I had to give it to him: From thirty meters, not bad.

The rest of his team opened fire on the other morons, who weren't quite the hard-core nihilists they expected.

"Team 2, push on. Now! We're almost there."

Elian's fighters jumped over the collection of bodies. The opia caravan and its wealth of targets lay in a clearing less than a hundred meters ahead.

On one hand, the advance was damned impressive. However, I saw the layout of our positions inside Elian's visor. Team 2 outpaced the other three by fifty meters. A final assault on the caravan needed to be comprehensive. Had he lost sight of the danger?

Moon recognized the problem.

"Team 2, hold position. Wait for reinforcement."

"Negative, boss. We're on top of this shit. 1, 3, and 4, whatcha waiting for?"

"Elian, I gave you an order. Hold until ..."

"Gotcha, boss, but we need to press the advantage. No worries. We'll soften up these malgados and leave the cleanup for you lot."

I wanted to reinforce Moon's orders, but interference through Ixoca was a dangerous distraction in the heat of battle. I had only myself to blame for what had become of Elian's combat exuberance.

The day I took him into space for the first time, I forced him to confess about his misguided past. He told me of the people he killed and the psychotic behavior that turned off the UNF and employers. After he unburdened, I gave him implicit permission to embrace his truth. I set the monster free. It was a specialty of mine.

Moon said, "Elian, halt. Now."

Elian's lieutenant tapped his shoulder.

"Sir, I'm picking up a new reading. It's ..."

An energy configuration dashed across the visor like a lightning bolt. Those weren't human signatures, nor were they above ground.

It happened before Elian could order his team to stop.

A chain of explosions tore out of the earth, spreading like a firewall. The concussion threw Elian back. The ground shook beneath him. But that didn't matter so much as the projectiles hurled in every direction.

Something lifted Elian into the air and slammed him to the ground.

He went dark for an instant. When he reopened his eyes, Elian stared upward at the thick canopy. His visor was cracked but functional, yet I only saw half the screen.

That's when I realized: One eye was out of commission.

The jungle went silent.

I recognized a faint gurgle. It was a desperate gasp for air, something I heard often on Swarm battlefields. Mouths open, lungs useless, words impossible. The final measure of a dying man ...

Shit.

"Elian?" I whispered. "Can you hear me? It's Raul."

"I ..." He managed nothing else.

"Elian, my friend. Listen to me. Ilan will be with you shortly. Don't try to move."

"Uh ... uh ... b ... boss. I ..."

"Don't talk, Elian."

"S ... sorr ... sorry."

I focused on Moon, who scampered through the battle zone at top speed. The second he entered Team 2's section of the attack grid, all enemy firing ceased. Elian's team had taken care of business quite nicely before they walked into a trap.

He ordered Teams 1 and 3 to deploy their rifters to Team 2's forward position.

"All others, continue the advance at half speed. Monitor for improvised devices."

Moon kept his head, but I heard a crack in his voice. Something was clawing its way out that I hadn't heard since before we ascended. Not since the early years, when he felt something other than a desire to kill and destroy. When he was still a boy.

He cared about a human. More than that, a genuine friend.

I wanted to intervene, to remind him not to allow this moment to blur his focus on the necessary task. OK, I'd been fond of Elian from the start. He greeted me that first day with such nerdish enthusiasm. Yes, he'd begun to lose his way, develop an ego the size of the Naugista Plateau.

And yet ...

I never imagined this moment. It always seemed pointless. Humans would follow us into fire, do as they were told, and die as needed. Failing that, they'd grow old, become useless, and die; we'd move on through the centuries. What was the point?

And yet, he *was* a friend. A human goddamn friend.

He mattered. He changed our trajectory. He made us rich. He was loyal. And shit if he weren't the life of every party.

Fuck me.

I knew he shouldn't have been out there. Moon, too. We lost our objectivity; we granted him a role he wasn't prepared to handle.

"I see him," Moon said.

The explosions had knocked the entire team to the ground, although several rose to their feet. But not the one who was decapitated or the one cut in half at the waist.

They too were loyal and followed us into fire, but I felt nothing for them. I'd seen worse during the war – my side *and* theirs.

As Moon approached Elian, I found my so-called heart conflicted. I considered filtering out the view. But this was my fault. My stupidity.

Two rifters arrived simultaneous to Moon, who stood over Elian.

The right side of his face drowned beneath blood and a gaping hole, inside of which something dark and blunt was buried. The eye wasn't there. Further down, a piece of shrapnel the shape of a spike cut open his left thigh. The leg was smashed at the knee. Everything below it curled up underneath. He'd never use that leg again ... assuming he lived long enough to need one.

"I got you, Elian," Moon told him. "We'll ... we'll fix this."

Moon lifted him onto the closest rifter. Three other soldiers, soon to bleed out, joined Elian.

"Maria, we have incoming. Prepare the phasic pods for four."

"On it, sir. Do we activate Backstop?"

We stationed two former UNF medics inside the Scramjet to handle non-life-threatening injuries on the ground at Ennoi. Anything that couldn't wait inside a trauma pod's stasis field for a few hours required an emergency flight to Desperido. That meant a forty-minute jump and preparation by a small team here. But even their skills were limited. I feared Elian exceeded their parameters.

"Yes," Moon said. "Backstop. Notify Desperido Control."

I intervened.

"I'm on it, my friend. We'll have everything in place."

He watched the rifters speed away toward the city.

"We fucked him over, Royal. He wasn't ready."

"I know, Moon. We'll do everything possible."

I heard the old rage return when he said:

"I'm going to finish it. I'll slaughter every malgado for fifty kilometers. I'll burn them out if I have to."

"No doubt, my friend. Take a moment, count our dead, consider the mission objective, and eliminate the *intended* targets. Concern yourself with scorched earth tomorrow."

I ran from my bunker at fifty times human speed and informed Bett of what happened long before word reached Desperido Control. I mentioned no names. If Elian did fall, the shock waves would not reverberate favorably through our army. The civilians, however, would take it far worse.

I stepped inside the adjacent conference room and gathered my thoughts. There were only two ways to restore Elian, assuming he survived the jump. Both came with a price.

After sucking in my pride, I deferred to Ixoca.

"The surgeon. We need him."

One of Ixoca's generals ran the largest trauma clinic in Marcon Province, nine hundred kilometers northwest of Desperido. I held off making the request until all other options failed. We purchased enough phasic medtools to handle most injuries, and I hoped to avoid falling further into debt with the mad Jewel.

"I see the surgeon's eyes," Ixoca said. "He is occupied with a medical consult. If I attempt to tear him away, he will ask many questions. Even then, he will have to travel by conventional means. I cannot promise to have him there any sooner than three hours."

"We'll make it faster. When Maria offloads the patients, you provide the coordinates, and we'll do the rest."

Red-pixelated Ixoca paused, which worried me.

"Many of my generals know about the activities in Desperido. They're aggressively engaged in protecting you. Dr. Nunes does not.

Once there, he will be compromised."

"Not a problem. I'll wipe his memory afterward."

"True, but you can't wipe mine. Royal, we agreed months ago: My children needed to remain at a distance unless I specified otherwise. You knew our compact might cost lives."

"Your point?"

"The time approaches where I will ask a favor in return."

I rolled my eyes.

"As you've often reminded me. Ixoca, if you want this favor done to your satisfaction, fulfill my request. Otherwise, I can't guarantee the job will meet your expectation."

That was the first time I threatened Ixoca. To my surprise, he responded in a congenial tone.

"We are partners in this journey. What kind of partner would I be to deny such a heartfelt request?"

"Thank you, Ixoca."

"You are quite welcome." He started to fade but added: "Royal, do you feel human? You sound like one."

I didn't dignify his insult with a response. Although Ixoca might have intended it as faint praise.

Human.

There was no rule that said a higher being couldn't show empathy and care for lesser creatures without becoming one.

No. I refused to let him get under my syneth.

Over the next several minutes, word spread of incoming wounded. We cleared a landing area outside Mod 3, where we installed our phasic medtools weeks ago. The synthetic blood tanks activated. After consulting with Bett and watching our forces on Indy Prime continue their march, we contacted Bart by deepstream.

They were offloading supplies at the Inuit facility and about to take on a small crew who finished their rotation. I canceled that part of their mission and ordered them to Ennoi. At thirty minutes, it was one of the shortest jumps in the Collectorate. They couldn't offer much; Bart's phasic capability was minimal. But we needed a second off-world ferry if the battle called for it.

When this crisis passed and Carlos upgraded the three Ladybugs to worm-capable status, I'd have to sit down with Moon and Bett to reorganize our fleet priorities. We should have known better.

Bett pulled me aside minutes before Maria exited aperture.

"Word will spread about Elian. If he dies, Raul …"

"He won't. That sorry malgado has too much to live for. All forty planets, I promised him."

"Great. Visions of an empire. Yeah. That'll save him. Why worry?"

"Leave the snark to me, Bett."

She rested hands on hips.

"Raul, he was barely alive when they locked him into stasis. That will keep his heart beating, but he can lose brain function. I saw it happen during the war. And our people can't work on him while he's in stasis."

"Nor will they."

"The fuck are you talk …?"

"We're collecting a specialist, courtesy of Ixoca. He'll provide the coordinates before Maria lands. We'll hold Elian in stasis an extra six to eight minutes. I want the news contained. Only Maria's crew and the medtechs are to know. They should focus their efforts on the other three. Understood?"

"Sure, Raul. I'll see it done."

I vowed not to distract Moon with updates when Elian arrived. Good or ill, the news was only bound to hinder the work. When Moon set his sights on a slaughter, best not to pull him off course.

Soon, Maria exited aperture and landed outside Mod 3. I jumped through the open egress and ordered the other soldiers be carried to the phasic center first.

I studied the life signs above Elian's stasis pod. Brain, heart, and lung functions were weak but stable. I saw him through the translucent lid. He was a disgusting mess, one side of his face

193

unrecognizable. Judging from the dents on his chest armor and helmet, he would have died instantly without them.

The surgeon needed to keep him alive, but *restoring* my young friend required a second option beyond human medical expertise. Moon and I long ago vowed we'd never do it. Not for a damn human.

No. One step at a time. Save the kid first, then talk syneth.

Two soldiers disconnected the pod, which hovered between them.

Maria's pilot, Sgt. Barden, asked about returning to Indy Prime.

"Negative, Sergeant. Take a break. I'll handle Nav."

"Sir?"

"I must make a pickup, my friend."

21

BLACK STAR LOST SEVEN FIGHTERS on Indonesia Prime. Five more were injured and still recovering after three days. We deployed one hundred and two in the battle to secure the Ularu Jungle. Some generals might have considered our kill rate acceptable given the nature of the enemy and the terrain. Not me.

The total exceeded our projections, which we most likely prepared with a healthy dose of arrogance. I wanted to lay the fault at our perfect record; it created the illusion of invincibility. Yet that was utter nonsense.

Men and women were always going to die in our employ. That was the goddamn point of Black Star. We brought death and chaos hidden behind the promise of prosperity and the illusion of new order. We would always fight enemies, some pitiable and others formidable. Our soldiers entered the fray as mere fodder to defend our brand with their lives.

If Black Star grew as we envisioned and the Collectorate fell to planetary uprisings, we'd kill millions through Motif and war. Our campaigns would reduce humanity to its most barbaric state in three thousand years. Generations of soldiers would rage and die under our banner. Everyone would know it was Moon and I who freed them from oppression, laws, regulations, and moral codes. We'd stand with the survivors as heroes.

At long last. Heroes.

So why did seven deaths bother me? Why did it send Moon on a continuous assault against the scum of Ularu for three days? Why did he ignore the Wak'inau's demand and order firebombs dropped from Maria until every human for twenty kilometers around Ennoi was ash?

When I was human, I walked over thousands of corpses on fields of battle. As unrestrained gods, my partner and I destroyed whole planets in another universe to teach the Swarm a lesson. We silenced billions of innocent songs.

So why did losing a few men and women bother me?

Eh.

I wasn't a moron. I knew the answer.

Saying it aloud wasn't an option.

Not yet.

Too much remained unresolved. Events unfolded at an accelerated pace. And then there was Ixoca.

Cudfrucking Ixoca! Our benefactor. In some ways, our hero. But a lunatic with an agenda waiting to be revealed.

Until we knew his mission and devised the perfect exit strategy with our *D'ru-shayas*, Moon and I were caught in a bind. I suppose that was always his plan.

I bounced from one dilemma to the next.

Several hours after the surgeon began tedious work on Elian, I sat in a strategy session with Bett. We discussed how to stabilize Ennoi, but Ixoca's many eyes led me to a place always of great interest.

Chief of Staff Kai Parke entered the President's office along with Leonard. The three had not met together since Leonard confronted me at 40-Cignus.

"We have a problem on Riyadh," Leonard said. "My contacts say the situation on the ground is changing rapidly."

The President grimaced. "Is this connected to Q6?"

"No. It's an internal matter, but the threat might be as great. Ahmed Faez has taken control of the Royal Guard."

Kai cursed. The President cupped a hand over her mouth.

"How did this happen, Leonard?"

"Mohandi Ra was accused of sexual indiscretions and forced out."

Kara laughed. "Of course he was. Not a word of it's true. I've known Mohandi for ten years. He was the best IC rep Riyadh ever had. Do your contacts know what Faez has in mind?"

"Uncertain. Some believe he wants the Emir's confidence. The Emir is old and not well. If Faez can convince him to reinstate the Rhulani Jihadists ..."

"No." Kara slammed the desk. "We are not going down that road again. We almost lost Riyadh twelve years ago. Faez hates me. He never forgave me for what happened during the negotiations."

"True, but there is hope. Some contacts believe Faez has reformed his views. They say he wants to serve the Emir in an honorable capacity. As a patriot."

Kai interjected. "Everyone's a patriot in their own mind. Madame President, regardless of his intent, one thing is clear: We need to open lines with the Emir."

The Prez tapped her fingers like a pianist.

"Yes. You're correct. I haven't spoken to him in two years. Didn't I promise to visit Riyadh City?"

Kai nodded. "There are only two planets you haven't visited. I'm sure it would go a long way to holding off a crisis."

"Good. Let's begin the process. This could take a while."

Leonard said, "Madame President, we could short-circuit the problem a different way. Our friends?"

"I'm open to all options."

They had me at *Riyadh*.

It was one of my least favorite worlds, though not without its share of natural wonders. I visited as an unrestrained god and didn't care a whit about their political fortunes. However, I knew Riyadh's importance in history.

More to the point: History *yet* to be made.

President Aleksanyan was going to die there. The continuum showed us no details about her assassination, only that it occurred in Standard Year 5390 on Riyadh. I had no idea who would stage it or why, and frankly didn't give a shit.

Except for the timing. If she was prepared to open diplomatic channels, then the visit would soon be added to her calendar. Weeks at most.

One era about to end. Another about to ...

No. I dared not get ahead of myself. Too many threads left to unspool. All our dreams might yet come undone.

At least one, however, remained alive and well.

More or less.

"I've done all I can for Elian," Dr. Arturo Nunes told me outside the surgery in Mod 3. "You'll need another specialist to finish the repairs, but even then ..."

"Yes. I understand. The damage was too extensive."

Nunes slept little since arriving. I gave him credit for persistence and professionalism. After three days with no outside contact allowed, he had run out of patience.

"Raul, I've seen miracles in this area, but facial reconstruction of the magnitude he requires will take years. Even that will not restore what he lost. Frankly, it's extraordinary he's alive, let alone cognizant of his surroundings."

"We have you to thank, my friend. You and our common ally."

He never mentioned Ixoca by name. Oh, these Children of Orpheus. They were a cagey lot.

"I have other patients and a family, Raul. Please allow me to return to them."

I thought of playing cagey as well, but it served no purpose.

"Your ride will leave in two hours. In the meantime, I excuse you from duty. Shower, eat, take a nap. Someone will call for you."

He frowned. This man smelled something rotten.

"That simple? I leave. No conditions."

"Won't be necessary. You'll have no memory of the past three days. I'm sorry, my friend, but you'll have to grapple with a hole in your mind."

He wanted to fight the decision, but Nunes was a smart man. I'm sure he knew the alternative would be far worse.

Permanent, actually.

"How will I explain it?"

"Ixoca has agreed to supply you with a story. He'll speak after we drop you off in a discrete location."

Nunes threw up his hands and walked away. Didn't blame the fella. On the other hand, he swore allegiance to an invisible creature that talked to him in his dreams. Crazy is as crazy does, I suppose.

Elian received a steady stream of well-wishers, but the dialogue was one-sided. His larynx suffered severe damage. He wouldn't talk for another week at the minimum. But he heard everyone, blinked his left eye, and shed a few tears, I heard. Many soldiers and civilians volunteered to nurse and feed him for the road to recovery ahead. He'd rarely find himself alone in the trauma cubicle.

Yet that's how I discovered him after dismissing Dr. Nunes.

A phasic trauma pod did almost everything except clean his ass and wipe his one viable nostril. The force shield immobilized his broken back. The holotools regulated his circulatory system, maintained the perfect body temperature, and repaired torn muscles and cartilage, fiber by fiber. They didn't concern themselves with his left leg, which no longer existed.

A separate program used nanodrones to stabilize the forty percent of his face that had been shorn away. Nunes operated four times, until he felt comfortable the NDs could take over. They worked beneath a magnetic blanket of sorts, hiding the disarray from view but keeping Elian's head immobile. Their program would run for five more days.

"Elian," I said inside his mind. The young kingpin's eye flickered open. "Hello there, my friend."

Elian could lick his lips, eat soft food, even smile on occasion. The temptation to push out words must have been fierce. He resisted.

"Hey, Raul. The doctor said he couldn't do anymore for me."

"Yes. You're alive because of his work, but the machines will take it from here. With good fortune, you'll be sitting and talking in eight or ten days."

He closed his eye.

"Are you sure? Everybody says the right things, but I think they don't wanna tell me the truth."

"Now, you wouldn't be accusing us of lying?"

"No. Not you, Raul. But the doctor. He looks at me like ..."

"Like there's a limit to his ability. He's only human, after all."

I thought that was humorous. Elian showed no reaction.

"Elian, your recovery is not up for debate. Quality of life afterward remains an open question."

The first time we conversed after he woke two days ago, I promised to hold nothing back. Damned if I would change my tune now.

"My leg."

I nodded. "Yes. You'll need a prosthetic. Dr. Nunes said the latest models have sufficient neural interfaces, although fitting will take time." I paused for dramatic effect. "Naturally, I didn't tell him who will provide your leg."

"You can create one?"

"Yes. I'll take the same approach as with Ship's arm. My syneth can generate one. I'll run a full scan of your right leg and set you up with a premium substitute. You and Ship will become syneth limb buddies."

There rose a smile.

"Ship came to visit last night. He tried to be supportive, but he couldn't look at me."

"The kid is sorting through a blend of psychoses. Give him time. Now, I came here because we need to discuss the one part of you that cannot be so easily replaced."

A tear ran down his cheek.

"The doctor said I'll never look the same again, but he wouldn't say how bad it is. Raul, I ..."

"Elian, it's dreadful. As in, death might have been a mercy. Nunes can't believe you survived. But he doesn't know you. Elian, you're a stubborn, psychotic, unbreakable and frustratingly optimistic son of a bitch. That, my friend, is why you live. But those qualities and the best human tech will not restore your face. Ever."

The next tears followed in a steady stream.

"Please, Raul. Tell me how bad it is."

"To be honest, I don't know the final result. The nanos are working beneath a shield. Let's put it this way. You'll have the benefit of something other humans don't: Two distinctly different faces. As an added bonus, you'll be able to scare little children."

He smiled and cried at once. I thought it was a nice quip.

"Or you can become a masked avenger. Very mysterious."

Eh. Enough bedside humor.

"Elian, I know what you want to ask, so I'll get right to it. My syneth can create complex objects. I pull from my reserves every time I do this. The objects must exist in my syneth matrix, which contains an inventory of literally millions of objects dating back ... well, long before I became a god.

"Unfortunately, you need reconstruction, not replacement. Even I can't screw off your head and replace it with a better one. Although that does sound promising." OK, so he appreciated the joke. "Elian, I can extract raw syneth, but there's a catch.

"If I program it to integrate with your genetic profile and reconstruct your face, it will have to engage with your brain. It will have to regenerate nerves, build an eye from scratch, reset half your teeth and your jawbone.

"It might work. In fact, I believe it will. For a short time, you will look like the Elian we knew. But syneth was not designed for permanent integration with organic creatures. The prosthetic limbs interact only at the point of contact. I don't know how far into your system the syneth will grow. No idea how if at all it will change you. If your body rejects it, you will die."

Elian quickly replied.

"But if it doesn't, I can be myself again."

"No, Elian. There you're wrong. You might look like your old self, but you won't be human. Not anymore. And before you ask: No, the syneth will not give you extended life or any special powers. You're mortal. You'll grow old and die like all the rest, my friend."

"But I'll see my empire grow, and I won't have to hide in the shadows like a goddamn monster."

That was one way for a narcissist to examine the problem. Couldn't expect one near-death experience to produce a personality reversal.

"The future is malleable. We'll face many obstacles before we can talk seriously about empires. Elian, you have time to consider your options. If you want to discuss it another day, I'll be around."

I wiped away his tears.

"Thank you, boss. Thank you for everything."

"Pleased to help. Always. You should rest."

As I turned to leave, he shouted in my mind.

"Raul, wait! I need to ask you a question."

"Yes?"

"Why haven't I heard from Ilan? All this time, he never touched my mind or came to visit."

Oh. That.

I avoided the extended truth.

"Ilan was your commander out there. He blames himself. But he's been trying to make right. Just today, he secured the last of the perimeter for Ennoi. I recalled him. He'll return after Tracer takes command of the mission. You're his first stop when he arrives."

Did Elian believe me? They'd become close friends, a surprisingly well-made pair of mass murderers.

"That's good to know, boss."

"Expect him in a few hours. Until then ..."

Elian interrupted me again.

"I'm sorry, boss. I'm sorry for everything. The last six months were the best of my life. I lost control. I'm sorry."

I smiled upon leaving the cubicle.

"We were all young once, my friend."

Perhaps his lack of judgment taught Elian a few lasting lessons. He might yet see the Motif empire grow. If so, I preferred he do it without my syneth integrated into his brain. Elian needed a physical reminder of his considerable hubris.

After I wiped Dr. Nunes of his recent memories, I cleared my own thoughts with a few drinks in the cantina then a walk around the perimeter. I closed off Ixoca's many eyes, except for my partner. Having so many in my head – most were ordinary, uninteresting stiffs – proved to be a lovely tool in the beginning. I felt closer to my old self. Now the endless monitors morphed into aggravating background noise. I wouldn't miss them after expelling Ixoca.

Of course, that assumed the process didn't kill us. Theo's plan was viable but required specific conditions. The odds, as they say, were not stacked in our favor.

Moon arrived on Maria five hours later. I asked him to join me on the western perimeter before he visited Elian. I came there often at sunset. It was the only time all day when I thought of nothing.

"Quite the slaughter, Moon. Tired?"

He sauntered beside me and lit a fresh cigar.

"I haven't been tired for two thousand years, Royal. Bored once in a while. Never tired."

"You submitted quite a report. Seven hundred dead."

"Estimate. The firebombs didn't leave much to pick through."

"Hmm. Lau Pot is annoyed with your tactics. Twenty percent of the eastern mountainside was burned."

"It's a goddamn jungle. It will grow back."

His cigar smoke blew in my face.

"And if Lau Pot continues to protest?"

"I'll kill him and install his Number Two."

"The son. Yes. I noticed how he seemed uninterested in daddy's traditional approach."

Moon grunted. "He'll do as he's told. He wants the credits."

I slapped my partner on the back.

"Outstanding! Ennoi seems in hand. Well done, my friend."

"How's Elian?"

"Improved. Long road ahead. Eager to see you. Moon, I ..."

He waved me off with a flick of his cigar.

"No. I won't talk about it."

"We must, my friend. It goes to the core of who we are."

"I'm aware. We will, but not today." He pulled hard on the cigar and cast a blue-white cloud toward the setting sun. "Royal, I got too close. Never again. Never again."

"Fair enough. We appear to be of similar mindset. We'll discuss when you're ready."

We watched the sun die in relative silence. Our mistake was the one we never saw coming, even after all the immaculate planning and exceptionally elaborate scheming.

Humans.

We allowed them in. We should have known better.

Moon tossed his half-smoked cigar on the red dust and sighed.

"I need to get it over with."

"Be gentle, my friend, assuming that's within your skillset."

Moon sneered. "It's not. Fortunately. I should have let him die."

"That's one school of thought. The other is ..."

A familiar voice interrupted me. I hated being interrupted.

"If I may," Ixoca said. It emerged out of the dying sunlight in full

204

gender-neutral form. "While I have you both together, I thought this a good time to touch base."

I gave Ixoca my best glad-to-see-you face.

"Oh?"

"First, I wanted to honor your achievements. Four off-world facilities, a thriving Desperido, and a larger worm-capable fleet. You're hitting all your marks. And young Elian is making a healthy recovery thanks to the surgeon I provided."

"We're grateful for the help, Ixoca."

The Jewel opened its arms like it wanted a hug.

"I was also pleased to hear your thoughts about losing objectivity with these humans. They can be useful, but we are not them and never will be. It's important to remember the hierarchy."

Moon crossed his arms. I felt his impatience, but he knew better than to antagonize our benefactor before we struck.

"What's your point, Ixoca?" Moon said with restraint.

"I must agree with my partner. You've often spoke of lifting up the Aztecan people to a greater destiny."

The Jewel appeared to smirk.

"I will. In fact, that's why I am here. It's time for you to repay my generosity. I trust you still intend to complete the mission at Conquillos Base."

Shit. That.

"Apologies, Ixoca. We've been busy the past few days. You still believe killing protestors when the UNF team arrives will advance your agenda?"

"Oh, yes."

Moon wanted to refuse, but he knew we needed to play along.

"If we do this," he asked, "what's next? The job at Conquillos is small change. You want more."

"*Much*, Moon. Happily, I intend to simplify the logistics for Black Star. The invitations have been sent. The final act is in motion."

"What invitations, my friend?"

"It will be a grand event. The first and last of its kind. Every one of my children will attend. Imagine! All members of the Children of Orpheus in one place. Do you know I've dreamed of this gathering for more than a thousand years?"

Definitely did not like the sound of that.

"What does it have to do with us?"

"Everything, Royal. You and Black Star will also attend."

"For what purpose?"

"To bear witness."

I hated obtuse assholes.

"Specifically, my friend?"

Ixoca considered us both then glanced skyward.

"What I started, you will finish. When we are done, Aztecans will fulfill a greater destiny. I call it White Sunset."

Nah. He wasn't insane at all.

"When?" Moon asked.

"Soon. I will make sure you have sufficient notice. I must say, fine gentlemen, this has been a gratifying partnership."

Ixoca shifted into red pixelation and turned toward the dusk.

"Hold for a moment, if you would."

"Yes, Royal?"

"Now that we stand on the edge of the precipice ... finally ... I have a question, though it's delicate."

Ixoca regained full form.

"I love delicate questions, my dear friend. Please."

"You speak of 'bearing witness.' Some time ago, Moon and I bore witness to the destruction of our home in the Fort of Inarra. You showed us the eyes of a Captain who ordered the attack. I long assumed the President or someone close to her sanctioned the mission. It was none of them."

"It wasn't, you say?"

The Jewel twisted its lips. Yes, it knew the punchline.

"You gave the order, Ixoca."

"I did."

The confession came without the hint of reservation. Huh.

"That Captain was one of your generals. It's interesting that he's no longer among the many eyes."

"A tragic loss. Fine man. His heart failed."

Now that's what I'd call damn convenient.

"Fragile humans," I said. "Even the healthy ones can drop dead. Am I right?"

"Indeed, Royal."

"One final question: Why destroy the fort?"

Ixoca reached out and laid his palms on our chests.

"The arrow points in one direction, but it must be guided with a steady hand."

I thought he'd say something to that effect. Obtuse asshole.

Oh, yeah. This was going to get nasty.

Will Royal and Moon extract themselves from Ixoca? What is the Jewel's plan for "White Sunset"? Will Black Star and Desperido survive what lies ahead? The story concludes now in Book 5: *White Sunset*.

Please feel free to drop a quick review of *Black Star* on Amazon before you race into the utterly bonkers final chapter of this saga.

Printed in Great Britain
by Amazon

63077777R00121